PENGUIN CLASSICS

Maigret's Patience

'Extraordinary masterpieces

'A brilliant writer'   – India Knight

'Intense atmosphere and resonant detail . . . make Simenon's
fiction remarkably like life'   – Julian Barnes

'A truly wonderful writer . . . marvellously readable – lucid,
simple, absolutely in tune with the world he creates'
                                                       – Muriel Spark

'Few writers have ever conveyed with such a sure touch, the
bleakness of human life'   – A. N. Wilson

'Compelling, remorseless, brilliant'   – John Gray

'A writer of genius, one whose simplicity of language creates
indelible images that the florid stylists of our own day can
only dream of'   – *Daily Mail*

'The mysteries of the human personality are revealed in all
their disconcerting complexity'   – Anita Brookner

'One of the greatest writers of our time' – *The Sunday Times*

'I love reading Simenon. He makes me think of Chekhov'
                                                       – William Faulkner

'One of the great psychological novelists of this century'
                                                       – *Independent*

'The greatest of all, the most genuine novelist we have had
in literature'   – André Gide

'Simenon ought to be spoken of in the same breath as
Camus, Beckett and Kafka'   – *Independent on Sunday*

ABOUT THE AUTHOR

Georges Simenon was born on 12 February 1903 in Liège, Belgium, and died in 1989 in Lausanne, Switzerland, where he had lived for the latter part of his life. Between 1931 and 1972 he published seventy-five novels and twenty-eight short stories featuring Inspector Maigret.

Simenon always resisted identifying himself with his famous literary character, but acknowledged that they shared an important characteristic:

> My motto, to the extent that I have one, has been noted often enough, and I've always conformed to it. It's the one I've given to old Maigret, who resembles me in certain points . . . 'understand and judge not'.

Penguin is publishing the entire series of Maigret novels.

GEORGES SIMENON

Maigret's Patience

Translated by DAVID WATSON

PENGUIN BOOKS

PENGUIN CLASSICS

UK | USA | Canada | Ireland | Australia
India | New Zealand | South Africa

Penguin Books is part of the Penguin Random House group of companies
whose addresses can be found at global.penguinrandomhouse.com.

First published in French as *La Patience de Maigret* by Presses de la Cité, 1965
This translation first published 2019
002

Copyright © Georges Simenon Limited, 1965
Translation copyright © David Watson, 2019
GEORGES SIMENON ® Simenon.tm
MAIGRET ® Georges Simenon Limited
All rights reserved

The moral rights of the author and translator have been asserted

Set in 12.5/15 pt Dante MT Std
Typeset by Jouve (UK), Milton Keynes
Printed and bound in Great Britain by Clays Ltd, Elcograf S.p.A.

ISBN: 978-0-241-30413-6

www.greenpenguin.co.uk

Penguin Random House is committed to a
sustainable future for our business, our readers
and our planet. This book is made from Forest
Stewardship Council® certified paper.

Maigret's Patience

1.

The day had begun like a memory from childhood: dazzling and flavoursome. For no particular reason, except that life was good, there was a smile in Maigret's eyes as he ate his breakfast. Madame Maigret's eyes were no less joyful as she sat opposite him.

The windows of the apartment were wide open, letting in the smells of the outside world, the familiar sounds of Boulevard Richard-Lenoir and the air, which was already warm and shimmering; a fine mist filtered the rays of the sun and made them almost palpable.

'Are you tired?'

He was surprised by the question and replied as he sipped his coffee, which seemed to taste so much better than on other days:

'Why should I be tired?'

'All that work you did yesterday, in the garden . . . You haven't used a spade or a rake for months.'

It was Monday, Monday 7 July. On Saturday evening they had taken the train to Meung-sur-Loire, to the little house they had been setting up for years, in anticipation of the day when, according to the regulations, Maigret was due to retire. In just over two years' time! At the age of fifty-five! As if a man of fifty-five, who has never really had a day's illness in his life and doesn't suffer from any infirmity, becomes overnight no longer capable of running the Crime Squad!

But what Maigret had the most trouble getting his head round was that he had lived for fifty-three years.

'Yesterday,' he corrected her, 'I was mainly asleep.'

'In full sun!'

'With my handkerchief over my face . . .'

What a splendid Sunday! A stew simmering in the low kitchen with its blue stone tiles, the scent of St John's Wort permeating the house, Madame Maigret bustling from one room to another, a scarf wrapped around her head because of the dust, Maigret in shirt-sleeves, his collar open, a straw hat on his head, weeding the garden, digging, hoeing, raking, and then finally dozing off after lunch and a glass of the local white wine in a red and yellow striped hammock chair where the sun soon shone on him, but without rousing him from his torpor . . .

On the train back home they both felt heavy and sluggish, their eyelids stinging, and they brought with them an odour that reminded Maigret of his childhood in the country, a mixture of hay, dried earth and sweat: the smell of summer.

'Another coffee?'

'I'd love one.'

Even his wife's apron with the small blue checks enchanted him with its freshness, its sheer simplicity, just as he was enchanted by the reflection of the sunlight in the panes of the dresser.

'It's going to be a hot day!'

'Very.'

He would open the windows that overlooked the Seine and work without his jacket on.

'What would you say to a lobster mayonnaise for lunch?'

It was good too to walk down the street, where the awnings of the shops formed rectangles of shade, good to wait for the bus, standing next to a young woman in a light dress on the corner of Boulevard Voltaire.

His luck was in. An old-style bus with a platform pulled up at his stop, so he could continue smoking his pipe as he watched the streets and the pedestrians gliding by.

Why did it remind him of the brightly coloured procession that had brought the whole of Paris on to the streets many years ago, shortly after he had got married, when he was still a timid young secretary in the local police station at Saint-Lazare? Some foreign sovereign and his plumed entourage were being driven in four-horse landaus while the helmets of the Republican Guard glittered in the sun.

Paris smelled the same as it did today; the light was the same, the feeling of languor the same. He wasn't thinking about retirement then. The end of his career, the end of his life seemed a long way off, too far off to worry about. Now here he was preparing a home for his old age!

No melancholy. Just a gentle smile. Le Châtelet. The Seine. An angler – there was always at least one – next to Pont au Change. Then lawyers in black gowns gesticulating in the courtyard of the Palais de Justice.

Finally, Quai des Orfèvres, of which he knew every stone, and from which he had nearly been banished.

Less than ten days earlier, a self-important prefect, who

didn't like policemen of the old school, had asked him to resign – take early retirement, as he had so elegantly put it – because of some misdemeanours the inspector was supposed to have committed.

Everything, or nearly everything, in the dossier he flicked through, was false, and for three days and nights, without being able to call on his colleagues for help, Maigret had tried to prove it.

Not only had he succeeded, but he had extracted a confession from the perpetrator of the plot, a dentist in Rue des Acacias, who had a number of crimes on his conscience.

But that was over and done with now. After saluting the two men on guard duty, he climbed the wide staircase, went into his office, opened the window, took off his hat and his jacket and stood contemplating the Seine and its boats while slowly filling a pipe.

Although his days were unpredictable, he had some almost ritualistic habits, things he did without thinking, like, once he had lit his pipe, going through the door into the inspectors' room.

There were some empty places among the typewriters and telephones, because the holidays had already begun.

'Morning, boys . . . Would you come in here a moment, Janvier?'

Janvier was leading the investigation into the thefts from jewellers' shops, more precisely from jewellers' windows. The last one had taken place the previous Thursday on Boulevard Montparnasse, using a method that had proved highly effective for more than two years.

'Anything new?'

'Hardly anything. Youngsters again: between twenty and twenty-five, according to witnesses. There were two of them, as usual. One smashed the window with a tyre lever. The other stuffed the jewels into a black cloth bag, soon helped by his comrade. It was all carefully orchestrated. A cream-coloured Citroën DS pulled up in the street next to them just long enough for the two men to jump in, then it disappeared into the traffic.'

'Handkerchiefs masking their faces?'

Janvier nodded.

'The driver?'

'The witnesses aren't all in agreement, but he seemed to be young as well, with very dark hair and a tanned complexion. Just one other lead, which may amount to nothing: a vegetable-seller noticed a short time before the burglary a broad-shouldered, shortish man with a boxer's face, standing just a few metres from the jeweller's as if he was waiting for someone. He kept looking up to check the time on the big clock above the shop window and then consulting his own watch. According to this woman, he never took his right hand out of his pocket. While the heist took place, he didn't move, but as soon as the cream-coloured car had gone, he hopped into a taxi.'

'Did you show the vegetable-seller the photos of the suspects?'

'She spent three hours with me in Records. But in the end she didn't formally identify anyone.'

'What did the jeweller say?'

'He was tearing out the few hairs he had left. He said

5

that if the theft had taken place just three days earlier it wouldn't have been that serious, because normally he doesn't have any really expensive jewellery on display. But last week he had the opportunity to buy a job lot of emeralds and on Saturday morning he decided to put them in the window.'

What Maigret didn't yet realize was that the events unfolding in his office that morning were the beginning of the end of a case that would henceforth be referred to at Quai des Orfèvres as Maigret's longest investigation.

Sometimes real events can, over the course of time, acquire the status of legend. 'Maigret's longest interrogation' was still much discussed, for example, and new comers to the department would hear all about it. It had lasted twenty-seven hours, during which the waiter from the Brasserie Dauphine had delivered a constant supply of beer and sandwiches.

Maigret wasn't the only one to grill the suspect. Lucas and Janvier took it in turns, each time starting the interrogation from scratch. Although this seemed very tedious, it did in the end produce a full confession.

Another thing that stuck in everyone's mind was 'Maigret's most dangerous arrest', the arrest of a gang of Poles, in the middle of a crowd, in broad daylight, without a single shot being fired, even though the men were armed to the teeth and were determined to save their skins.

Arguably, the business of the jewels started for Maigret twenty years earlier, when he became interested in a certain Manuel Palmari, a Corsican crook who had started small as a pimp.

There was a changing of the guard at that time. The old bosses, who before the war owned brothels, ran secret gambling dens and organized spectacular burglaries, had retired one after the other, to the banks of the Marne or to the South of France, and for the less lucky and less clever ones to the prison in Fontevrault.

The youngsters, who imagined they would tear everything up, moved in and took over. They were more audacious than the old guard, and for several months the police were wrong-footed and kept at bay.

This was the beginning of the attacks on debt collectors and the jewellery heists in broad daylight with lots of people around.

Eventually some of the culprits were arrested. The crimes stopped for a period of time, flared up again, decreased once more, and then restarted with a vengeance two years later.

'The kids we arrest are just the footsoldiers,' Maigret had stated from the beginning of these raids.

Not only were there new faces each time, but those whom they arrested mostly didn't have a police record. They weren't from Paris either. They appeared to have come up from the provinces, particularly Marseille, Toulon and Nice, for a specific job.

Once or twice only they went for the large jewellers on Place Vendôme and Rue de la Paix, but these had the deterrent of alarm systems.

They quickly changed their tactics. Now they targeted small jewellers, no longer in the centre of Paris, but further out, even in the suburbs.

'Well, Manuel?'

Ten times, a hundred times, Maigret had questioned Palmari, first at the Clou Doré, the bar he had bought on Rue Fontaine and turned into an upmarket restaurant, then later at the apartment he shared with Aline on Rue des Acacias. Manuel had never made an issue about this, and they might have passed for two old friends having a get-together.

'Sit down, inspector. What can I do for you?'

Manuel was now nearly sixty and, since he had been shot by a machine gun while lowering the shutter at the Clou Doré, confined to a wheelchair.

'Do you know a young man who was born on your island, a nasty piece of work called Mariani?'

Maigret filled his pipe; this always took a while. In the end he came to know every nook and cranny of the apartment on Rue des Acacias, especially the little corner room, full of cheap novels and gramophone records, where Manuel spent his days.

'What's he done, this Mariani? And why is it, inspector, that I am always the one who gets pestered about these things?'

'I've always been straight with you, haven't I?'

'That's true.'

'I've even done you one or two favours.'

That too was true. Without Maigret's intervention, Manuel would have found himself in a spot of bother on more than one occasion.

'If you would like that to continue, tell me more . . .'

So Manuel did: in other words, he named names.

'You know, it's just a guess. I'm not involved and I have a clean record. I don't know this Mariani personally. I've just heard tell . . .'

'By whom?'

'I don't know, just a rumour going round . . .'

Since the shooting incident, when he had lost a leg, Palmari rarely received visitors. He knew his telephone was tapped and he was careful only to make calls that would not attract suspicion.

Moreover, for the last few months, since the jewel robberies had started up again, there were two inspectors permanently stationed in Rue des Acacias – two, because one had to follow Aline wherever she went while his partner continued to keep an eye on the building.

'OK . . . Just as a favour . . .'. There is an inn near Lagny, I can't remember the name, kept by an old man who is half deaf and his daughter. I think Mariani is keen on the girl and likes staying at the inn.'

Yet every time in the last twenty years Manuel had shown signs of having come into some money, this had coincided with an upsurge in jewellery thefts.

'Have they found the car?' Maigret asked Janvier.

'In a sidestreet near Les Halles.'

'Any fingerprints?'

'Nothing. Moers went over it with a fine-tooth comb.'

It was time for the briefing in the commissioner's office, and Maigret joined the other divisional heads.

Each of them summed up their cases in progress.

'And what about you, Maigret? How's it going with the jewel thefts?'

'Do you know, sir, how many jewellers there are in Paris, not to mention the inner suburbs? More than three thousand. Some of them only sell cheap jewels and watches, but you could say that roughly a thousand of them have something on display that would tempt an organized gang.'

'What's your conclusion?'

'Let's take the jeweller's on Boulevard Montparnasse. For months it had only low-grade stock on display. By chance the other week the owner got hold of some expensive emeralds. On Saturday morning he thought he would put them on display. On Thursday his window was smashed and the jewels were stolen.'

'Do you suppose . . .?'

'I'm almost certain that a man in the trade does a tour of the jewellers' shops, sometimes moving to a different neighbourhood. Someone is alerted whenever any nice pieces are displayed in a suitable location. Then they bring up from Marseille or somewhere some youngsters who have learned the ropes but who aren't yet on the police's radar. On two or three occasions I've set traps by asking jewellers to display some rare pieces.'

'But the gang haven't fallen for it?'

Maigret shook his head and relit his pipe. He merely mumbled:

'I am patient.'

The commissioner, however, was not so patient and made no secret of the fact that he was far from happy.

'And this has been going on . . . how long?'

'Twenty years, sir.'

A few minutes later Maigret got back to his office, pleased to have kept his cool and his good humour. Once again he opened the door to the inspectors' room, because he hated using the internal telephone.

'Janvier!'

'Coming, chief. I've just received a phone call . . .'

He came into Maigret's office and shut the door.

'Something unexpected has happened . . . Manuel Palmari . . .'

'Don't tell me he's disappeared.'

'He's been killed. Shot several times in his wheelchair. The chief inspector from the seventeenth arrondissement is on the scene and he has informed the prosecutor's office.'

'What about Aline?'

'It seems she was the one who called the police.'

'Let's go.'

At the door, Maigret turned back to grab a fresh pipe from his desk.

As Janvier drove the small black car up the Champs-Élysées in a halo of light, Maigret still had the faint smile on his lips and the twinkle in his eyes that he had woken up with and which he saw too on the lips and in the eyes of his wife.

Nevertheless, deep down he felt not exactly sad, but somewhat nostalgic. Manuel Palmari's death would not be universally mourned. Apart from – though this was far from certain – Aline, who had lived with him for several years and whom he had picked up from the street, and a few crooks who owed him everything, most were likely to mark his passing with: 'He had it coming.'

One day Manuel had told Maigret that he had been a choirboy too in his home village, a village so poor, he went on, that young people left it at the age of fifteen to escape from the misery. He had wandered round the docks in Toulon, where he later worked as a barman and quickly learned that women constituted a capital that could bring in a good income.

Did he have one or more crimes on his conscience? Some hinted at it, but nothing was ever proved, and then one day Palmari became the proprietor of the Clou Doré.

He thought he was cunning, and it was the case that up until the age of sixty he had ducked and dived so successfully that he had never been convicted.

True, he hadn't managed to dodge the machine-gun bullets, but in his wheelchair, among his books and his records, his radio and his television, he still had a zest for life, and Maigret suspected he loved even more passionately and tenderly his little Aline, who called him 'Daddy'.

'You shouldn't have seen the inspector, Daddy. I know the cops and they've always given me a hard time. This one is no better than the rest. Just you wait, one day he'll take the information he's got out of you and use it against you.'

She would sometimes spit on the ground between Maigret's feet, and then strut off with her head held high, wiggling her firm little behind.

It had only been ten days since Maigret had left Rue des Acacias, and now here he was again, on his way back to the same house, in the same apartment where, standing next to the window, he had had a sudden flash of inspiration that had enabled him to piece together the crimes of the dentist opposite.

There were two cars parked outside the building. A uniformed officer was posted in front of the door and when he saw Maigret he raised his hand to his cap.

'Fourth floor on the left,' he murmured.

'I know.'

The local chief inspector, a certain Clerdent, was on his feet in the living room talking to a small chubby man with very fair dishevelled hair, skin as white as a baby's and innocent blue eyes.

'Hello, Maigret.'

Seeing Maigret was looking at his companion and was unsure whether to hold out a hand, he added:

'You two don't know each other? . . . Detective Chief Inspector Maigret, this is Examining Magistrate Ancelin.'

'A pleasure to meet you, inspector.'

'The pleasure is all mine, sir. I've heard a lot about you, but I haven't yet had the honour of working alongside you.'

'I was only appointed to Paris about five months ago. I was in Lille for a long time.'

He had a falsetto voice and, despite his plumpness, seemed much younger than his age. He was more like one of those perpetual students who are in no hurry to give up their easy Left Bank lifestyles. Easy, that is, for those who have a rich daddy.

He was dressed sloppily, his jacket was too tight, his trousers too wide and baggy round the knees and his shoes could have done with a good polish. The word at the law courts was that he had six children, that he wasn't the master of his own house, that his old car was in danger of falling to bits at any moment and that to make ends meet he lived in a low-rent apartment.

'As soon as I had telephoned the Police Judiciaire I alerted the prosecutor's office,' the local chief inspector explained.

'Has the deputy arrived?'

'He'll be here in a minute.'

'Where is Aline?'

'The girl who lived with the victim? She's face down on the bed, crying her eyes out. There's a cleaning woman in there taking care of her.'

'What did she say?'

'I didn't manage to get much out of her and, given the state she's in, I didn't push it. She claims she got up at seven thirty. The cleaner only came at ten o'clock in the morning. At eight o'clock, Aline took Palmari his breakfast in bed then gave him a wash.'

Maigret knew the domestic routine here. Since the shooting that had left him an invalid, Manuel had not dared get into a bath. He stood under the shower on his one leg and Aline soaped him and then helped him put on his underwear and clothes.

'What time did she leave?'

'How do you know she left?'

Maigret would be sure once he had asked the two officers

on guard on the street. They hadn't telephoned him. No doubt they had been surprised to see the local chief inspector arrive, then the examining magistrate, then Maigret himself, since they were unaware of what was going on inside the building. There was something ironic in that.

'Excuse me, gentlemen.'

A tall young man with a long face came bursting in, shook everyone's hands and asked:

'Where's the body?'

'In the room next door.'

'Any leads?'

'I was just telling Inspector Maigret what I know. Aline, the young woman who lived with Palmari, claims she left the building around nine o'clock, without a hat, carrying a string shopping bag.'

One of the officers downstairs would surely have followed her.

'She went to various shops in the neighbourhood. I haven't yet taken down a written statement, as she had trouble stringing her words together.'

'So it was when she was out that . . .'

'So she claims . . . She says she came back at nine fifty-five.'

Maigret looked at his watch, which said 10.50.

'She found Palmari in the room next door. He had slipped out of his wheelchair to the floor. He was dead and had lost a lot of blood, as you will soon see.'

'What time was it when she telephoned you? I was told that it was she who telephoned the police station.'

'Yes, it was. It was ten fifteen.'

The deputy, Alain Druet, asked the questions while the chubby magistrate was happy just to listen, a vague smile on his lips. He too, despite struggling to feed his kids, seemed to enjoy life. Every now and again he cast a furtive glance at Maigret as if to share a certain complicity. The other two, the deputy and the local chief inspector, talked and behaved in a manner befitting conscientious public servants.

'Has the doctor examined the body?'

'He just popped in and out again. He says it's impossible until we have a post-mortem to determine how many bullets Palmari received. Impossible too, without undressing him, to distinguish the entry and exit wounds. However, the bullet that went through his neck seems to have come from behind.'

So, Maigret thought, Palmari didn't see it coming.

'Gentlemen, shall we have a quick look before Criminal Records get here?'

Manuel's little room looked no different, and it was flooded with sunlight. On the floor lay a body twisted into an almost absurd shape, with fine white hair stained with blood at the nape of the neck.

Maigret was surprised to see Aline Bauche standing against the curtain of one of the windows. She was wearing a light-blue linen dress that he recognized; her black hair framed her pale face, which was marked with red blotches, as though someone had struck her.

She was looking at the three men with such an expression of hatred or defiance that it seemed as if she was about to pounce on them with her claws out.

'Well, Monsieur Maigret, I trust you're satisfied now?'

Then, addressing all of them:

'So I'm not allowed to be alone with him, like any other woman who has just lost the man in her life. I expect you're going to arrest me now, aren't you?'

'Do you know her?' the examining magistrate whispered to Maigret.

'Fairly well.'

'Do you think she did it?'

'They must have told you that I never think anything, sir. I'm waiting for the men from Criminal Records to come with their equipment. Would you allow me to question Aline on my own?'

'Do you want to take her away?'

'No, I prefer to do it here. I can tell you anything I learn straight away.'

'When the body is removed perhaps we should seal the doors of this room.'

'The local chief inspector will see to that, if you don't mind.'

The magistrate still looked at Maigret with mischievous eyes. Is this how he had imagined the famous inspector? Was he disappointed?

'I'll give you a free hand, but keep me up to date.'

'Come with me, Aline.'

'Where are you taking me? Quai des Orfèvres?'

'Not that far. To your room. Janvier, go and fetch our men who are stationed outside and all three of you wait for me in the living room.'

Aline watched the specialists invade the room with a hard stare.

'What are they going to do with him?'

'The usual. Photographs, fingerprints, etc. By the way, has the weapon been found?'

She pointed to a table next to the sofa where she would lie for days at a time, keeping her lover company.

'Was it you who picked it up?'

'I didn't touch it.'

'Do you recognize this automatic?'

'As far as I know, it belongs to Manuel.'

'Where did he keep it?'

'In the daytime, he hid it behind the radio; at night he kept it on his bedside table.'

A Smith & Wesson .38, a professional's gun, a merciless weapon.

'Come, Aline.'

'What for? I don't know anything.'

Reluctantly, she followed him into the living room and opened the door to a very feminine bedroom, with a huge low bed like something from the movies rather than a Parisian interior. The curtains and hangings were of buttercup silk; a huge white goatskin rug covered most of the floor, and the net curtains transformed the light into golden dust.

'I'm listening,' she said peevishly.

'So am I.'

'This could take a while.'

She sank into an armchair of ivory silk. Maigret didn't dare sit on any of the delicate chairs and wasn't sure whether he should light his pipe.

'I am sure that you didn't kill him, Aline.'

'Seriously?'

'Don't be sarcastic. You helped me last week.'

'Not the cleverest thing I've ever done in my life. The proof of that is your two men permanently stationed on the pavement across the street. The tall one even followed me this morning.'

'I'm just doing my job.'

'Don't you ever feel disgusted by it?'

'How about a truce? Let's just agree that I do my job and you do yours and it doesn't matter if we end up on opposite sides of the fence.'

'I've never hurt a soul.'

'Maybe so. On the other hand, someone has just hurt Manuel irreparably.'

He could see her eyelids puff up with tears, and they seemed genuine. She blew her nose clumsily, like a little girl trying to suppress her sobs.

'Why should . . .'

'Why should what?'

'Nothing. I don't know. Why must he be dead? Why did they pick on him? As if he wasn't unhappy enough with only one leg and being stuck indoors all the time.'

'He had your company.'

'That caused him pain too, because he was jealous, though God knows he had no reason to be.'

Maigret picked up a gold cigarette case from the dressing table, opened it and offered it to Aline. She mechanically took a cigarette.

'You came back from your shopping trip at nine fifty-five?'

'The inspector will confirm that.'

'Unless you gave him the slip, as you manage to do from time to time.'

'Not today.'

'So there was no one you needed to contact on Manuel's behalf, no instructions to give, no telephone call to make?'

She shrugged her shoulders and automatically wafted the smoke away.

'Did you come up the main staircase?'

'Why would I have used the back stairs? I'm not a servant.'

'You went to the kitchen first of all?'

'Yes, as I always do when I get back from the market.'

'May I see?'

'Open that door. It's directly opposite in the corridor.'

He gave it just a quick glance. The cleaner was making coffee. There were vegetables strewn over the table.

'Did you empty your string bag?'

'I don't think so.'

'You aren't sure?'

'It's one of those things you do without thinking. Considering what happened afterwards, I have trouble remembering.'

'Knowing you, you then went into Manuel's room to give him a kiss.'

'You know as well as I do what I found.'

'What I don't know is your exact movements.'

'First, I think I cried out. Instinctively I rushed over to him. Then I have to admit, when I saw all this blood I recoiled in horror. I couldn't even bring myself to give him a last kiss. Poor Daddy!'

The tears began to flow, and she didn't think of wiping them away.

'Did you pick up the gun?'

'I've already told you I didn't. You see! You make out you believe me, and no sooner are we alone together than you start setting nasty traps.'

'You didn't touch it, not even to wipe it?'

'I didn't touch a thing.'

'When did the cleaner arrive?'

'I don't know. She uses the back stairs and never disturbs us when we are in this room.'

'You didn't hear her come in?'

'You can't hear anything from the little room.'

'Does she sometimes arrive late?'

'Frequently. She has a sick son whom she has to tend to before she comes here.'

'It was ten fifteen before you rang the police station. Why was that? And why wasn't your first thought to call a doctor?'

'You saw the state of him, didn't you? How many people who are alive look like that?'

'What did you do in the twenty minutes between finding the body and making the telephone call? A word of advice, Aline. Don't answer straight away. I know you. You have often lied to me, and I haven't challenged you about it. I'm not sure the examining magistrate will be as well disposed as me. And he is the one who decides whether you walk free or not!'

She put on her best street-girl sneer and said:

'That would take the biscuit! Arrest me! And people

still believe in justice. Do you still believe in it, after what happened to you? Tell me, do you believe in it?'

Maigret preferred not to answer.

'You see, Aline, those twenty minutes may be crucially important. Manuel was a cautious man. I don't think he would have kept compromising papers or objects in this apartment, still less jewels or large sums of money.'

'What are you getting at?'

'Can't you guess? Normally when you discover a body the first thing you do is call a doctor or the police.'

'I guess I just don't have the same reactions as normal people.'

'You didn't just stand there in front of the body for twenty minutes.'

'For a while, at least.'

'Doing nothing?'

'If you must know, first of all I prayed. I know it's stupid, since I don't even believe in their precious God. But there are times when it all comes back to you, in spite of yourself. Whether there was any point or not, I prayed for his soul to rest in peace.'

'And then?'

'I walked.'

'Where?'

'From the little room to this room and from this room to the door of the little room. I was talking to myself. I felt like a caged animal, like a lioness who had just had her mate and her cubs taken away from her. Because he was everything to me, my husband and child rolled into one.'

She spoke passionately, striding round the room as if reconstructing her actions of the morning.

'That all took twenty minutes?'

'Maybe.'

'It didn't occur to you to inform the cleaner?'

'I didn't even think about her. At no point was I even aware of her presence in the kitchen.'

'Did you leave the apartment?'

'To go where? Ask your men.'

'All right. Let us assume you are telling the truth.'

'That's exactly what I'm doing.'

She could act like a good girl on occasion. Perhaps she was good deep down and her attachment to Manuel was a sincere one. Only, as with many others, her experiences had made her bad-tempered and aggressive.

How could she believe in goodness and justice and trust people after the life she had had before she met Palmari?

'We're going to try a little experiment,' Maigret muttered as he opened the door.

He called out:

'Moers! Can you come and bring the paraffin?'

It now looked as if the apartment had been taken over by removal men, and Janvier, who had brought along Inspectors Baron and Vacher, didn't know where to put himself.

'Wait a moment, Janvier. Come in, Moers.'

The specialist had understood and was preparing his instruments.

'Your hand, please, madame.'

'Why?'

Maigret explained:

'To establish whether or not you fired a gun this morning.'

Without batting an eyelid, she held out her right hand. Then, just in case, they repeated the experiment on the left.

'When can you let me know the result, Moers?'

'About ten minutes. I've got everything I need downstairs in the van.'

'Is it true that you don't suspect me, and all this is just routine?'

'I am more or less certain that you didn't kill Manuel.'

'Then what do you suspect me of?'

'You know that better than I, my dear. I'm in no hurry. It will come out in due course.'

He called Janvier and the two inspectors, who were looking ill at ease in this yellow and white bedroom.

'Over to you, boys.'

As if getting ready for a fight, Aline lit a cigarette and puffed out the smoke with an expression of disdain.

2.

When he had left home, Maigret wasn't expecting to go back to Rue des Acacias, where he had spent so many anxious hours a week earlier. He was just setting out on another radiant day just like a few million other Parisians. He was expecting even less to be sitting with Examining Magistrate Ancelin around one o'clock in the afternoon in a bistro called Chez l'Auvergnat. It was across the road from Palmari's building and was an old-fashioned bar with a traditional zinc counter top, aperitifs that no one but old people drank any more and a landlord in a blue apron, with his shirt-sleeves rolled up and a resplendent black moustache.

There were sausages, salamis, cheeses shaped like gourds, hams with greyish rinds as if they had been kept in ash, all hanging from the ceiling, and in the front window there were enormous flat loaves of bread from the Massif Central.

Through the glazed door to the kitchen, the landlady could be seen working at her stove, thin and gaunt.

'Is it for lunch? A table for two?'

There was no tablecloth, but just some embossed paper on top of oilcloths on which the landlord added up the bills. The menu was chalked on a board:

Rillettes du Morvan
Rouelle de veau aux lentilles
Fromage
Tarte maison

The chubby magistrate lit up in this ambience, hungrily inhaling the thick aroma of cooking. There were no more than two or three silent customers, regulars whom the landlord knew by name.

For months this had been the headquarters of the inspectors who took it in turn to keep an eye on Manuel Palmari and Aline, one of them on standby to follow the young woman when she left the building.

For the time being, their work seemed to be at an end.

'What's your opinion, Maigret? Mind if I call you that, even though we've only just met? Though, as I said earlier, I have been looking forward to meeting you for a long time. Do you know that I find you fascinating?'

Maigret merely muttered:

'Do you like veal?'

'I like all country dishes. I too am the son of peasants. My older brother runs the family farm.'

Half an hour earlier, when Maigret had emerged from Aline's room, he had been surprised to find the magistrate waiting for him in Palmari's little room.

By then Moers had made his preliminary report to Maigret. The paraffin test had been negative. In other words, it wasn't Aline who had pulled the trigger.

'There were no fingerprints on the gun, which was

carefully wiped, or on the door handles, including the front door to the apartment.'

Maigret frowned.

'You mean that the handle didn't even have Aline's fingerprints?'

'That's right.'

She chipped in:

'I always put gloves on when I go out, even in summer, as I hate having damp hands.'

'Which gloves did you wear this morning when you went out for your walk?'

'Some white cotton gloves. Here! These ones.'

She took them out of a handbag shaped like a holdall. Some green marks showed that she had been handling vegetables.

'Baron!' Maigret called.

'Yes, chief?'

'Was it you who followed Aline this morning?'

'Yes. She left a little before nine o'clock and she was carrying a red string shopping bag as well as the handbag over there on the table.'

'Was she wearing gloves?'

'White gloves, as usual.'

'You didn't let her out of your sight?'

'I didn't go inside the shops, but I never lost her from view.'

'Did she make any telephone calls?'

'No. At the butcher's she queued up for quite a while but didn't talk to any of the other women who were waiting.'

'Did you note what time she got back?'

'To the minute. Nine fifty-four.'

'Did she seem to be in a hurry?'

'Quite the opposite. She gave me the impression she was dawdling and smiling, like someone enjoying the nice weather. It was already hot, and I noticed sweat marks under her arms.'

Maigret was sweating too and could feel his shirt getting damp, even though his jacket was quite light.

'Call Vacher. Good. Tell me, Vacher, while your colleague was following Aline Bauche, did you stay at your post outside the building? Where were you standing?'

'In front of the dentist's house, just opposite, except for a five-minute break when I had a glass of white wine at the Auvergnat's. You can see the front door of the building very well from the bar.'

'Do you know who went in and out?'

'First I saw the concierge, who came to shake out a rug on the doorstep. She spotted me and muttered something or other, because she doesn't like us watching the building and takes it as a personal insult.'

'Then?'

'Around nine ten a young woman left with a portfolio under her arm. It was Mademoiselle Lavancher; her family lives on the first floor on the right. Her father works as an inspector on the Métro. She goes every morning to an art school on Boulevard des Batignolles.'

'And afterwards? Did anyone go in?'

'The butcher's boy delivered some meat, I don't know to whom. I'm familiar with him because I always see him at the butcher's up the road.'

'Anyone else?'

'The Italian woman on the third floor beat her carpets out of the window. Then, a few minutes before ten, Aline returned with a load of shopping, and Baron came back and joined me. We were surprised when the local chief inspector turned up later, then the examining magistrate, then yourself. We didn't know what to do. We thought that, awaiting further instructions, we'd better stay in the street.'

'By early afternoon I'd like a complete list, floor by floor, of all the tenants in the building, with details of their families, professions, habits, etc. Get on to it, the pair of you.'

'Should we question them?'

'I'll handle that myself.'

Manuel's body had been taken away, and the pathologist was no doubt beginning the post-mortem.

'Aline, I have to ask you not to leave the apartment. Inspector Janvier will stay with you. Have your men gone, Moers?'

'They've finished their work here. We'll have the photos and an enlargement of fingerprints by about three o'clock.'

'So there were some fingerprints after all?'

'All over the place, as usual: on the ashtrays, for example, on the radio, the TV, the records and any number of objects that the murderer probably didn't touch and so didn't think it necessary to wipe.'

Maigret frowned, and that is when he noticed that Ancelin was scrutinizing his every change of expression.

'Do you want me to send out for some sandwiches, boys?'

'No, we'll go and have lunch after you.'

On the landing, the magistrate asked:

'Are you going home for lunch?'

'Unfortunately no, even though there's a lobster waiting for me.'

'Would you like to join me?'

'You don't know the neighbourhood as well as I do. Allow me to invite you, if you don't mind eating Auvergnat food in a bistro.'

And so they ended up at this table with the paper tablecloth, Maigret occasionally taking out his handkerchief to mop his brow.

'I presume that you consider the paraffin test conclusive, Maigret? I did once study scientific methods of investigation, but I confess I don't remember a lot about it.'

'Unless the murderer was wearing rubber gloves, there will certainly be minuscule traces of powder on their hands which will last two or three days and which the paraffin test will reveal without fail.'

'Don't you think that, given that the cleaner only comes for a few hours a day, Aline might wear rubber gloves, if only to do the washing-up?'

'It's likely. We'll soon find out.'

He began to look at the little magistrate with curiosity.

'These rillettes are splendid. They remind me of the ones we made on the farm when we slaughtered the pig. As I understand it, Maigret, you prefer to conduct your investigations alone, I mean just you and your colleagues, and to wait until you get some results before sending your report to the prosecutor's office and the examining magistrate.'

'We can't really do that any more. All suspects have the right to have a lawyer with them even at the first interrogation. The lawyers don't much like the atmosphere at Quai des Orfèvres and feel more at ease in front of a magistrate.'

'I didn't stay behind this morning and come to lunch with you simply to keep an eye on what you are doing, believe me, still less to rein you in. As I told you, I am curious about your methods and will learn a lot by watching you at work.'

Maigret gave no reply to this compliment other than a vague shrug.

'Is it true you have six children?' he asked in turn.

'It will be seven in three months' time.'

The magistrate's eyes were laughing, as if he were playing a huge joke on society.

'You know, it's very educational. From a very early age children have the qualities and faults of grown-ups, so you get to know individuals by watching them live.'

'Does your wife . . .'

He was about to say: 'Does your wife agree with you?'

But the magistrate continued:

'My wife's dream is to be Mother Rabbit in her hutch. She is never happier and more carefree than when she is pregnant. She gets enormous, puts on up to thirty kilos, but she carries it easily.'

A jolly, upbeat examining magistrate sampling the fillet of veal with lentils in an Auvergnat bistro as if he ate there every day.

'You knew Manuel quite well, didn't you?'

'Almost twenty years.'

'Was he a tough guy?'

'Both tough and tender, it's hard to say. When he arrived in Paris, after bumming around Marseille and the Côte d'Azur, he was ruthless and ambitious. Most of his sort soon become acquainted with the police, the courts, the assizes, prison.

'Although Palmari frequented that circle, he kept his head down and when he bought the Clou Doré, which was only a bistro at the time, he didn't need too much convincing to give us information about his customers.'

'He was one of your informers?'

'Yes and no. He held us at arm's length, fed us just enough to keep on our right side. For example, he always made out that he didn't see the two men who shot him as he was about to lower his shutters. Coincidentally, two hit-men from Marseille were shot dead in the South of France a few months afterwards.'

'Did he get on well with Aline?'

'He saw everything through her eyes. Make no mistake: despite her origins and her early experiences, this girl is someone to be reckoned with. She is far more intelligent than Palmari was and with the right sort of management she could have made a name for herself on the stage or screen. She could have turned her hand to anything.'

'Do you think she loved him, despite the age difference?'

'Experience has taught me that for women, for some of them at least, age doesn't matter.'

'So you don't think she committed the murder this morning?'

'I suspect no one and everyone.'

There was only one other customer in there eating, and two others at the bar, workmen who were on a job in the neighbourhood. The fillet of veal was delicious, and Maigret couldn't remember having eaten such succulent lentils. He made a note to come back here one day with his wife.

'Knowing Palmari, the gun would have been in its usual place behind the radio this morning. If Aline didn't kill him, then the murderer was someone Manuel trusted implicitly, probably someone who had a key to the apartment. But in the months that the building has been under surveillance, Palmari hasn't received any visitors.

'You'd have to pass through the living room, whose door is always open, go into the little room and walk round the wheelchair to get to the gun. If it was a villain, he knew all about the paraffin test. But I can't see Palmari receiving a visitor who was wearing rubber gloves. Finally, my officers didn't see anyone enter the building. When questioned, the concierge hadn't seen anyone either. There is a butcher's boy who makes deliveries every day at the same time, but he can be discounted.'

'Someone might have got into the building yesterday evening or last night and stayed hidden on the stairs?'

'That's something I intend to look into this afternoon.'

'You said earlier that you had no idea. Would it annoy you if I suggested you had something approaching an idea at the back of your mind?'

'You're right. Only, it may lead nowhere. The building

has five floors, not counting the ground floor and the attic. There are two apartments on each floor. So there must be quite a few tenants.

'For months, all of Palmari's telephone calls were recorded, and they were all perfectly innocent.

'I've never bought the fact that this man had withdrawn from the world completely. I had Aline followed every time she went out.

'That's how I discovered that she made telephone calls from the back room of a shop she used.

'She also sometimes managed to give my men the slip for a few hours, using the classic trick of a building with two entrances – a department store or the Métro.

'I have the dates of these telephone calls and these escapes. I have compared them to the dates of the jewellers' shops burglaries.'

'Do they match up?'

'Yes and no. Not always. Often the telephone calls took place five or six days before a burglary. The mysterious escapes, on the other hand, sometimes happened just hours after the thefts. Draw your own conclusions, bearing in mind that the heists were nearly all carried out by young men with no previous record who had come up especially from the South or from the provinces. Would you like some more tart?'

It was a juicy plum tart, flavoured with cinnamon.

'If you'll join me.'

They washed down their meal with a brandy with no label which must have been at least 65 per cent proof and brought a flush to their cheeks.

'I'm beginning to understand,' the magistrate sighed as he too began to mop his brow. 'A shame that I have to get back to the office and can't follow your investigation step by step. Do you know what you're going to do next?'

'I have no idea. If I did have a plan I would be forced to change it in a few hours. For now I will concentrate on the tenants in the building. I'll go round like a door-to-door salesman selling vacuum-cleaners. Then I'll drop in on Aline again. She hasn't told me everything yet and will have had time to reflect. That doesn't mean that she will be any more forthcoming than this morning.'

After a brief argument about the bill, they got up to leave.

'I invited myself,' the magistrate protested.

'I'm almost on home ground here,' Maigret insisted. 'It will be your turn next time.'

The landlord called out from behind the counter:

'Enjoy your meal, gents?'

'Very much.'

So much, in fact, that they both felt a bit heavy, especially once they had emerged into the glare of the sun.

'Thanks for the lunch, Maigret. Remember to keep me up to date.'

'I promise.'

And as the florid magistrate slipped behind the wheel of his decrepit car, Maigret once more entered the building with which he was becoming increasingly familiar.

He had eaten well. He still had a taste of the brandy in his mouth. The heat, even though it made him drowsy, was pleasant; the sun was full of joy.

Manuel liked good meals and a good brandy too, and these fine, sleepy summer days.

He was probably now lying under a rough sheet in one of the metal drawers of the Forensic Institute.

Baron paced about the room, whistling. He had taken off his jacket and opened the window, and Maigret guessed that he was in a hurry to get something to eat, though only once he had downed a large beer.

'You can go. Leave your report on my desk.'

Maigret noticed Janvier, also in shirt-sleeves, in the little room, where he had lowered the Venetian blinds. When Maigret came in, he stood up, replaced the popular novel he was reading on the bookshelves and grabbed his jacket.

'Has the cleaner gone?'

'I questioned her before she left. She isn't very talkative. She's new, taken on at the start of the week. The old one has gone back to the provinces – Brittany, I think – to look after her sick mother.'

'What time did she arrive today?'

'Ten o'clock, according to her.'

In Paris, as elsewhere, there are different types of cleaners. This one, who was called Madame Martin, was the most disagreeable type, those women who have suffered misfortune and continue to be a magnet for disaster and bear a grudge against the world as a whole.

She wore a black dress that had become shapeless and down-at-heel shoes and she stared at people suspiciously, with a fierce look in her eyes, as if she was always anticipating being attacked.

'I don't know anything,' she had told Janvier before he had even opened his mouth. 'You have no right to pester me. I've only worked here four days.'

You could tell she was in the habit of muttering vengeful phrases under her breath as she went about her solitary work.

'I'm off, and no one can stop me. I'll never set foot here again. I suspected they weren't married and that it would all end in tears.'

'What makes you think that Monsieur Palmari's death had something to do with them not being married?'

'That's how it is, isn't it?'

'Which staircase did you come up?'

'The servants' one,' she replied bitterly. 'There was a time, when I was younger, when they would have been happy to let me come up the main staircase.'

'Did you see Mademoiselle Bauche?'

'No.'

'Did you go straight into the kitchen?'

'I always go there first.'

'How many hours a day are you here?'

'Two hours, from ten until twelve. The whole morning on Mondays and Saturdays, except now I won't ever be here on a Saturday, thank God.'

'What did you hear?'

'Nothing.'

'Where was your mistress?'

'I don't know.'

'Didn't you ask her for instructions?'

'I'm old enough to know what to do after I've been told once.'

'And what were you supposed to do?'

'Put away the shopping she had just brought in and left on the table. Then wash the vegetables. Then vacuum the living room.'

'Did you have time to do it?'

'No.'

'What did you do next on the other days, after the living room?'

'The bedroom and the bathroom.'

'Not the little room?'

'The gentleman's study? The young lady looked after that herself.'

'You didn't hear any shots?'

'I didn't hear anything.'

'Or your mistress's voice talking on the telephone?'

'The door was closed.'

'What time did you see Mademoiselle Bauche this morning?'

'I don't know exactly. Ten or fifteen minutes after I got here.'

'How was she?'

'She'd been crying.'

'She wasn't still crying?'

'No, she said: "Don't leave me on my own. I'm afraid I might faint. They've killed Daddy." '

'And then?'

'She headed for the bedroom, and I followed her. It was only when she threw herself on the bed that she started crying again. Then she said to me: "When the doorbell rings, answer it. I've called the police." '

'Were you not curious enough to ask for more details?'

'I don't concern myself with people's business. The less I know, the better.'

'You didn't go and take a look at Monsieur Palmari?'

'What would be the point?'

'What did you think of him?'

'Nothing.'

'What about her?'

'Same. Nothing.'

'You've been here since Monday. Have you ever seen anyone visit?'

'No.'

'Has anyone asked to speak to Monsieur Palmari?'

'No. Is that all? Can I go now?'

'As long as you leave me your address.'

'I am not far away. I live in a garret in the most run-down house on Rue de l'Étoile, number 27A. You'll only find me there in the evening, because I'm cleaning all day. And remember that I don't like the police.'

Janvier had just read Maigret this statement, which he had typed up.

'Has Moers been gone long?'

'About three-quarters of an hour. He's searched the whole place, examined the books one by one, the record sleeves. He asked me to tell you that he found nothing. No secret hiding place in the walls either, no double drawers in the furniture. He vacuumed the rooms just in case and took away the dust for analysis.'

'Go and get some lunch. I recommend the fillet of veal at Chez l'Auvergnat, if they're still serving at this time.

Then come back afterwards and pick me up. Did you advise the local chief inspector not to say anything to the press?'

'Yes. Just now. By the way, that magistrate wasn't on your back, was he?'

'No, quite the opposite. I'm already beginning to like the man.'

Once he was alone, Maigret took off his jacket, slowly filled his pipe and started to look around, as if taking possession of the place.

Palmari's wheelchair, which he hadn't seen unoccupied before, suddenly looked ominous, especially as the leather on the seat and the back still bore the imprint of Palmari's body and the hole made by one of the bullets, which had lodged itself in the padding of the back.

He randomly picked up some books, some records, and turned on the radio for a moment, which blared out an advert for a brand of baby food.

He raised the blinds at the windows, one of which looked out on to Rue des Acacias, the other on to Rue de l'Arc-de-Triomphe.

For three years, Palmari had lived in this room from dawn to dusk, leaving it only to go to bed, after Aline had undressed him like a child.

According to what he had said ten days earlier, which the inspectors had confirmed, he never received visits, and apart from the radio and the television, his companion was his only link with the outside world.

Finally, Maigret crossed the living room and knocked on the bedroom door. When he got no response he opened it and found Aline lying on her back in the huge bed, staring at the ceiling.

'I hope I didn't wake you?'

'I wasn't asleep.'

'Have you eaten?'

'I'm not hungry.'

'Your cleaner says she's not coming back.'

'What do I care? If only *you* wouldn't come back.'

'What would you do?'

'Nothing. If you were ever shot dead, would your wife appreciate having her apartment invaded and being asked question after question?'

'Unfortunately, I have to do it.'

'I can't think of anything crueller.'

'Except the murder itself.'

'And you suspect me of it? In spite of the test your specialist did this morning?'

'I presume you do the cooking?'

'Like all women who don't have a maid.'

'Do you wear rubber gloves?'

'Not for cooking, but to peel the vegetables and do the washing-up.'

'Where are they?'

'In the kitchen.'

'Will you show me?'

She got up grudgingly, her eyes dark with spite.

'Come.'

She had to open two drawers before finding them.

'There! You can send them to your artists. I didn't wear them this morning.'

Maigret put them in his pocket without a word.

'Contrary to what you might think, Aline, I have a lot of sympathy and even a certain admiration for you.'

'Am I supposed to be touched by this?'

'No. I would like you to come and have a chat with me in Manuel's room.'

'If I don't . . . ?'

'What do you mean?'

'If I refuse? I suppose you'll take me to your office at Quai des Orfèvres?'

'I'd rather do things here.'

She shrugged her shoulders, walked in front of him and slumped down on the narrow sofa.

'Do you think it will upset me to see where the crime took place?'

'No. It would be better if you stopped being so tense, so much on the defensive and hiding what you will be forced to admit to me one day.'

She lit a cigarette and looked at Maigret indifferently.

Pointing to the wheelchair, the inspector murmured:

'You want whoever did this to be punished, don't you?'

'I'm not counting on the police.'

'You'd rather take care of it yourself? How old are you, Aline?'

'You know. Twenty-five.'

'So you have your whole life ahead of you. Did Manuel leave a will?'

'I never bothered to find out.'

'Did he have a lawyer?'

'He never mentioned one.'

'Where did he keep his money?'

'What money?'

'To start with, what he earned from the Clou Doré. I know it is you who received the money due to Manuel from the manager each week. What did you do with it?'

She looked like a chess player weighing up her next move and all the possible consequences.

'I put the money in the bank and kept only what I needed for the housekeeping.'

'Which bank?'

'The branch of the Crédit Lyonnais on Avenue de la Grande-Armée.'

'Is the account in your name?'

'Yes.'

'Is there another account in Palmari's name?'

'I don't know.'

'Listen, Aline. You're an intelligent girl. Up until now, with Manuel, you've led a certain type of life, pretty much on the margins of society. Palmari was a gang leader, a tough guy, who made himself respected for years.'

She pointed ironically at the wheelchair, then at the still-visible bloodstain on the carpet.

'If a man like him, who knew all the ropes, gets himself killed, what do you think will happen to a young and now defenceless woman?

'Do you want to know what I think? I think there are only two possibilities. Either those who went after him will come after you next and they will be just as success-ful. Or they will leave you alone, and that will tell me you are in league with them.

'You see, you know too much, and in these circles the accepted opinion is that only the dead don't talk.'

'Are you trying to scare me?'

'I'm trying to concentrate your mind. We've been playing games too long, you and I.'

'Which would prove, according to your theory, that I am able to keep quiet.'

'Would it bother you if I opened the window?'

He opened the one that wasn't in direct sunlight, but the air from outside was barely cooler than that in the room, and Maigret continued to sweat. He couldn't decide whether to sit down or not.

'For three years you lived here with Manuel, who, as both you and he claimed, had no contact with the outside world. In fact, he did have contacts, with you as his intermediary.

'Officially, you went once a week, occasionally twice, to check the takings at the Clou Doré, collect Palmari's share and deposit the money in the bank, in an account registered under your name.

'But you often felt the need to give my officers the slip, either to make mysterious telephone calls or to give yourself a few hours of freedom.'

'Maybe I had a lover.'

'And it doesn't bother you even a bit saying something like that on a day like today?'

'It's just to show you that there are any number of possibilities.'

'No, my girl.'

'I'm not your girl.'

'I know! You've told me umpteen times. It doesn't mean

there aren't times when you act like a kid and I feel like giving you a slap.

'I said just now that you are intelligent. But you don't seem to grasp what sort of hornet's nest you've stumbled into.

'Adopting this attitude while Palmari was there to advise you and protect you is one thing. But now you are all alone, do you understand? Is there any other weapon in the house other than the one the experts are currently looking at?'

'Kitchen knives.'

'You want me to go, and not keep an eye on you any more . . .'

'That's exactly what I want.'

He shrugged his shoulders, discouraged. Nothing had any effect on her, despite her obvious dejection and an anxiety she couldn't completely conceal.

'Let's approach this from a different angle. Palmari was sixty. For fifteen years he was the proprietor of the Clou Doré, which he ran himself until his infirmity prevented him. From his restaurant alone he earned a lot of money, and he had other sources of income.

'Now, apart from buying this apartment, paying for the furniture and the running costs, he didn't spend a lot of money. So where is the fortune he accumulated?'

'It's too late to ask him.'

'Do you know his family?'

'No.'

'Don't you think that, loving you as much as he did, he would have arranged for this money to pass to you?'

'You said it, not me.'

'People like him generally avoid putting their money

in banks, because it is too easy to check the dates the deposits were made.'

'I'm still listening.'

'Manuel didn't work alone.'

'At the Clou Doré?'

'You know that's not what I'm talking about. I mean the jewels.'

'You've been here at least twenty times to ask him about that. And did you get anything out of him? So why do you think, now that Daddy's dead, you'll get anything more out of me?'

'Because you are in danger.'

'Is that any concern of yours?'

'I wouldn't like to go through this morning's ceremony again for you.'

It seemed to Maigret that she was beginning to have second thoughts, but nevertheless, as she stubbed out her cigarette in the ashtray, she sighed:

'I have nothing to say.'

'Then in that case you will allow me to have one of my men in your apartment day and night. Another will continue to follow you when you go out. Finally, I have to request officially that you don't leave Paris until this investigation is over.'

'I get it. So where will your inspector sleep?'

'He won't sleep. If you ever feel the need to tell me anything, telephone me at my office or call me at home. Here is my number.'

She didn't take the card he offered her, so eventually he left it on the table.

'Now that our conversation is over, can I offer you my very sincere condolences? Palmari may have decided to live on the margins of society, but I can't deny that I had a sort of admiration for him.

'Goodbye, Aline. That's your doorbell, and it is almost certainly Janvier coming back from lunch. He'll stay here until I send another inspector to relieve him.'

He was about to hold out his hand to her. He could sense she was troubled. Knowing she wouldn't respond to the gesture, he put on his jacket and went to the door to let Janvier in.

'Anything to report, chief?'

He shook his head.

'Stay here until I send a replacement. Keep an eye on her and mind the back stairs.'

'Are you going back to the office?'

Maigret made a vague shrug and sighed:

'I don't know.'

A few minutes later, he was drinking a large beer in a bar on Avenue de Wagram. He would have preferred the atmosphere in Chez l'Auvergnat, but there was no phone booth in the bistro. The telephone there was on the wall next to the counter, where the other customers could eavesdrop on your conversation.

'Another beer, please, waiter and a few telephone tokens. Make it five.'

A rather thick-set prostitute smiled at him naively, without realizing who he was. He took pity on her and signalled to her that he wasn't interested and not to waste her time.

3.

Staring idly through the glass of the phone booth at the customers sitting round the tables, Maigret first of all called Ancelin, the examining magistrate, to ask him to delay sealing off the room on Rue des Acacias.

'I left one of my men in the apartment and I'll be sending another soon to do the night shift.'

'Have you questioned the young woman again?'

'I've just had a long conversation with her, but no joy.'

'Where are you right now?'

'In a bar on Avenue de Wagram. I have a few more calls to make.'

He thought he heard a sigh. Was the chubby magistrate jealous of him, out there in the throbbing heart of the city while he sat in a dusty office poring over abstract files and following monotonous routines?

At school, Maigret used to gaze longingly out of the classroom window at all the men and women coming and going in the street while he remained shut up inside.

The bar was almost full, and it still surprised him after all these years to see people out and about at times of the day when others were beavering away in offices, workshops and factories.

When he first arrived in Paris, he could spend whole afternoons on a café terrace on the Grands Boulevards or

48

on Boulevard Saint-Michel, watching the crowd flow by, observing the faces and trying to guess what was on everyone's minds.

'. . . Thank you. If there are any more developments I'll update you as soon as possible.'

Next, he rang the pathologist, whom he managed to reach in his surgery. Doctor Paul wasn't there any more; his young replacement was a less colourful character but was conscientious in his work.

'As you know, your men found a bullet lodged in the back of the wheelchair. It was fired from in front, when the victim was already dead.'

'From what distance, roughly?'

'Less than a metre but more than fifty centimetres. I can't be more precise than that without resorting to guess-work. The bullet that killed Palmari was fired from behind, in the neck, almost from point-blank range, at a slight upward angle, and it lodged itself in the cranium.'

'Were the three bullets of the same calibre?'

'As far as I can tell. Ballistics are examining them now. You will receive my official report tomorrow morning.'

'One last question: what time?'

'Between nine thirty and ten o'clock.'

Next, Gastinne-Renette.

'Have you had time to examine the gun I brought you and the three bullets?'

'I just have to run some checks, but it is almost certain at present that the three bullets were fired from a Smith & Wesson.'

'Thank you.'

Out in the bar, a shy man was circling round before finally plucking up the courage to sit down next to the prostitute with the thick hips and the over-made-up face. Without looking at her, he ordered a beer and showed his embarrassment by tapping his fingers on the tabletop.

'Hello! Fraud Squad? Maigret here. I'd like to speak to Detective Chief Inspector Belhomme, please.'

Maigret seemed more interested in what was going on in the room than by what he was saying.

'Belhomme? Maigret here. I need your help, old fellow. It's concerning a certain Manuel Palmari, who lives, or rather lived, on Rue des Acacias. He is dead. Some of his little friends decided that he had outstayed his welcome. Palmari owned a restaurant on Rue Fontaine, the Clou Doré, which he handed over to a manager about three years ago.

'Did you get that? He lived with a certain Aline Bauche. She has an account in her own name at the branch of the Crédit Lyonnais on Avenue de la Grande-Armée. It seems that she deposited a portion of the Clou Doré takings there every week.

'I have reason to believe that Palmari had access to more substantial sources of revenue. We found nothing at his apartment except a few thousand- and hundred-franc bills in his wallet and roughly two thousand francs in his mistress's handbag.

'I don't need to draw you a diagram. The stash must be somewhere, perhaps in the possession of a lawyer, perhaps invested in a company or in property. I could be wrong, but I believe it is a large amount . . .

'Yes, urgent, as always. Thanks, old man. See you tomorrow.'

Then a call to Madame Maigret, like the one he had made that morning.

'I don't think I'll be home for dinner, and it's possible I may not be home until late . . . Now? . . . Avenue de Wagram, in a bar . . . What will you have to eat? . . . A herb omelette? . . .'

Finally, to the Police Judiciaire.

'Put Lucas on the line, will you? . . . Hello! Lucas? . . . Can you come straight away to Rue des Acacias? . . . Yes . . . Organize a night shift to take over from you at eight . . . Who's available? . . . Janin? . . . Perfect . . . Warn him he will have to stay awake all night . . . No, not outside . . . He'll have a comfortable armchair.'

The young man stood up, his cheeks crimson, and followed the woman, who was old enough to be his mother, as she weaved her way between the tables and chairs. Was it his first time?

'Waiter, a beer.'

Outside, the air was sizzling, and the women looked like they weren't wearing anything under their light dresses. If the self-important prefect could see Maigret now, wouldn't he have accused him again of doing work inappropriate for a departmental head?

Nevertheless, this is how Maigret had succeeded in the majority of his investigations: by climbing stairs, sniffing round in dark corners, chatting to all and sundry and asking what at first seemed like pointless questions, spending hours in bars, not all of them entirely salubrious.

The little magistrate had understood that and envied him.

A few minutes later, Maigret entered the lodge of the building where Aline lived. Concierges are like cleaners: all good or all bad. He had met some who were charming, neat and easy-going, whose lodges were models of order and cleanliness.

This one, who must have been around fifty-five, belonged to the other category, that of the crabby ones, always complaining about their health problems and ready to blame their sad lot on the wickedness of the world.

'You again?'

She was shelling peas, a cup of coffee in front of her on the oilcloth that covered the round table.

'What else do you want from me? I've already told you that I didn't see anyone go up, apart from the butcher's boy who has been delivering here for years.'

'I suppose you have a list of the tenants?'

'How else could I collect all the rents? If only everyone paid the day it is due! When I think that I have to go up four or five times to see people who don't want for anything!'

'Could you give me the list?'

'I don't know if I should. It would be better if I asked the landlady first.'

'Does she have a telephone?'

'Even if she didn't have one, I wouldn't have far to go.'

'She lives here in the building?'

'Really? Are you making out you don't know her? Oh well, too bad if I'm out of order. Now's not the time to bother her, because she has enough worries as it is.'

'You mean . . . ?'

'You didn't know? No matter! You'd have found out one day. Once the police start sniffing around . . . Yes, it's Mademoiselle Bauche.'

'The receipts are filled out in her name?'

'Who else's name, since the building belongs to her?'

Without being asked, Maigret chased the cat from the wicker chair and sat down.

'Let me see the list.'

'On your own head be it. You'll have to sort it out with Mademoiselle Bauche, and she is not always easy to deal with.'

'Is she tight with money?'

'She doesn't like it when people don't pay, not to mention her moods.'

'I see that the apartment next to yours is occupied by someone called Jean Chabaud. Who is he?'

'A young man, barely twenty, works in television. He is nearly always away travelling, because he mainly covers sports: football, motor racing, the Tour de France . . .'

'Married?'

'No.'

'Does he know Aline Bauche?'

'I don't think so. I was the one who got him to sign the lease.'

'And the apartment on the right?'

'Can't you read? There's a nameplate on the door: Mademoiselle Jeanine Hérel, chiropodist.'

'Has she lived in the building for long?'

'Fifteen years. She's older than me. She has lots of clients.'

'First floor on the left, François Vignon . . .'

'Is it a crime to be called Vignon now?'

'Who is he?'

'He works in insurance, married, two children. The youngest is only a few months old.'

'What time does he leave the building?'

'Around eight thirty.'

'In the apartment on the right, Justin Lavancher.'

'Inspector on the Métro. He starts work at six in the morning and wakes me up as he walks past the lodge at five thirty. A right grumbler with a bad liver. His wife is so stuck up. They should keep an eye on that daughter of theirs; she's just turned sixteen.'

Second floor on the left: Mabel Tuppler, an American woman, around thirty, lives on her own, writes articles for newspapers and magazines back home.

'No, she doesn't see any men. Men leave her cold. Unlike women . . .'

On the same floor, on the right, a retired couple in their sixties, the Maupois, formerly in the shoe business, and their maid Yolande, who lives upstairs in the garret. Three or four times a year the Maupois treat themselves to a trip to Venice, Barcelona, Florence, Naples, Greece or somewhere similar.

'What do they do with their days?'

'Monsieur Maupois goes out around eleven to drink his aperitif, always dressed to the nines. In the afternoon, after his nap, he accompanies his wife on a walk or to do some shopping. If they weren't so stingy . . .'

Third floor. On one side a certain Jean Destouches, PE teacher at a school at Porte Maillot. Goes out of the house at eight o'clock in the morning, often leaving his girlfriend of the previous week or the previous night asleep in his bed.

'It's like a revolving door up there. How can he do sport when he doesn't get to sleep until two o'clock in the morning?'

'Do Destouches and Aline Bauche know each other?'

'I've never seen them together.'

'Was he here before she became the owner of the building?'

'He only moved in last year.'

'Have you ever seen Mademoiselle Bauche visiting his landing, going in or out of his door?'

'No.'

On the right, Gino Massoletti, the French representative of an Italian car company. Married, with a very pretty wife.

'Butter wouldn't melt in her mouth,' the concierge added between gritted teeth. 'And as for their maid, who lives up in the garret along with the Lavanchers' maid, she's like a bitch in heat. I have to let her in after hours at least three times a week.'

Fourth floor: Palmari, the late Palmari rather, to the left, and Aline. On the same landing, the Barillards.

'What does Fernand Barillard do?'

'He's a travelling salesman. He works for a luxury packaging firm: chocolate boxes, paper cones for sugared almonds, boxes for bottles of perfume. Last New Year he gave me a bottle of perfume and some *marrons glacés* that can't have cost him a penny.'

'What age? Married?'

'Forty to forty-five. Quite a pretty wife, buxom, always laughing, a very blonde Belgian woman. She sings all day long.'

'Do they have a maid?'

'No. She does the housework and the shopping. She goes to a tea room every afternoon.'

'Is she a friend of Aline Bauche?'

'I've never seen them together.'

On the fifth floor, Tony Pasquier, second barman at Claridge's, his wife and two children, aged eight and eleven. A Spanish maid who lives in the garret alongside the other three maids in the building.

In the apartment on the right, an Englishman, James Stuart, a bachelor, who never goes out before five in the afternoon and doesn't return until the early hours. A man of independent means. A cleaner comes in the late afternoon. Frequent trips to Cannes, Monte Carlo, Deauville, Biarritz and, in winter, various Swiss resorts.

'Any relations with Aline Bauche?'

'Why do you keep asking about everyone in the building having relations with her? And what do you mean by "relations" anyway? Do you think they sleep together? None of the tenants even knows she is the landlady.'

In any case, Maigret put a cross next to the Englishman's name, not because he had any connection to the present investigation, but because he might be a client of the Police Judiciaire one day. The Gambling Squad, for example.

That left the sixth floor, the garret. The four maids, from right to left: Yolande, who worked for the Maupois couple on the second floor; Massoletti's Spanish woman; the Lavanchers' maid; and finally Tony the barman's maid.

'Has Stuart lived in the building long?'

'Two years. He took the apartment over from an Armenian rug seller and bought all his furniture and fittings.'

Another inhabitant of the garret was Mademoiselle Fay, who was known as Mademoiselle Josette, an old lady who was the longest-standing tenant in the building. She was eighty-two years old and still did her own housework and shopping.

'Her room is full of birds in cages, which she puts on the window-sill in turn. She has at least ten canaries.'

An empty room, then the room of Jef Claes.

'Who's he?'

'A deaf and dumb old man who lives on his own. In 1940 he escaped from Belgium with his two married daughters and his grandchildren. As they were waiting in northern France, in Douai I believe, for a refugee train to come and take them away, the station was bombed, and there were more than a hundred casualties.

'Most of his family was wiped out. He himself received wounds to the head and face.

'One of his sons-in-law was killed in Germany; the other remarried in America.

'He lives alone and never goes out except to buy food.'

The peas had all been shelled a long time ago.

'Now I'm hoping you will leave me in peace. I'd just like

to know when the body will be returned and the funeral will take place. I should make a collection among the tenants to buy a wreath.'

'We can't be certain as yet.'

'There's someone over there who seems to be looking for you . . .'

It was Lucas, who had just come into the building and was standing outside the lodge.

'Police. I can smell them at ten paces.'

Maigret smiled.

'Thank you!'

'I only answered your questions because I had to. But I'm not a snitch, and if everyone just minded their own business . . .'

As if to purify the lodge of the imaginary fumes that Maigret had left there, she went and opened the window that looked out on the courtyard.

'What are we going to do, chief?'

'We're going upstairs. Fourth floor on the left. Janvier must be dreaming about a cool glass of beer. That is, unless Aline has taken pity on him and offered him one of the bottles I spotted in her fridge this morning.'

When Maigret rang the bell of the apartment, Janvier answered the door with a strange expression on his face. Maigret understood why once he had gone into the living room. Aline was leaving out of the other door, the one leading to the bedroom. In place of the light-blue dress she had on that morning she was wearing an orange silk négligé. On a side-table there were two glasses, one of them half full, some bottles of beer and some playing cards which had just been dealt out.

'Look, chief, it's not what you think,' Janvier said somewhat defensively.

Maigret's eyes were laughing. He casually counted the hands of cards.

'Belote?'

'Yes. Let me explain. When you left I insisted that she should have something to eat. She didn't want to listen and shut herself in her room.'

'Did she try to make a telephone call?'

'No. She lay on her bed for about three-quarters of an hour and then reappeared in a dressing gown, looking agitated, like someone who has been struggling to get to sleep.

' "Look, inspector, what's the point of me being at home if I'm simply a prisoner?" she said to me. "What would happen if I decided to go out?"

'I thought I was right to reply: "I won't prevent you, but an inspector will follow you."

' "Are you intending to stay all night?"

' "Not me. One of my colleagues."

' "Do you play cards?"

' "Sometimes."

' "How about a round of belote to pass the time? That would help take my mind off things." '

'By the way,' Maigret told Lucas, 'you should telephone headquarters and get one of our men to come and stand guard outside the building. Someone good at not being given the slip.'

'Bonfils is there. He's the best at this sort of thing.'

'He'd better let his wife know he won't be home tonight. Where is Lapointe?'

'At the office.'

'Tell him to come and wait for me here. Have him come up and stay with you until I get back. Do you play belote, Lucas?'

'I can hold my own.'

'Aline will be calling on your services too.'

He knocked on the bedroom door, which opened immediately. Aline must have been listening.

'Forgive me for disturbing you.'

'You seem to regard this place as your own. I'm not wrong, am I?'

'I simply wish to put myself at your disposal in case you need to contact anyone. There will be nothing in the papers until tomorrow at the earliest. Would you like me, for example, to inform the manager at the Clou Doré about what happened? The lawyer, perhaps, or family members?'

'Manuel didn't have any family.'

'And you?'

'They don't care about me any more than I care about them.'

'If they knew you were the owner of a building like this they would come to Paris in a flash, don't you think?'

She took that on the chin and didn't respond or ask him how he knew.

'Best wait until tomorrow to contact an undertaker; you don't yet know when the body will be returned to you. Do you want us to bring him back here?'

'This is where he lived, isn't it?'

'I suggest you eat something. I'll leave Inspector Lucas with you, whom you know. If there is anything at all you want to say to me, I'll be in the building for a while longer.'

This time the young woman gave him a sharper look.

'In the building?'

'I thought I'd like to meet the tenants.'

She kept her eyes on him as he dismissed Janvier.

'I'll send someone to take over around eight or nine o'clock, Lucas.'

'I had Janin lined up, but I'd rather stay myself, if someone could bring up some sandwiches.'

'And beer . . .'

Lucas pointed at the empty bottles.

'Unless there are more in the fridge.'

For nearly two hours Maigret went through the building from top to bottom and from one end to the other: polite, patient but as obstinate as a door-to-door salesman.

Gradually the names given him by the concierge ceased to be abstractions and became shapes, faces, eyes, voices, attitudes – actual human beings.

The chiropodist on the ground floor could have been mistaken for a card-reader, with her very pale face devoured by almost hypnotic dark eyes.

'Police? Why? I haven't done anything wrong in my life. Ask my clients – I've been caring for them for nine years.'

'Someone in the building has died.'

'I saw a body being taken out, but I was busy at the time. Who is it?'

'Monsieur Palmari.'

'I don't know him. Which floor?'

'The fourth.'

'I've heard the name mentioned. He has a very pretty wife, though she has a few airs and graces. I've never seen him. Was he young?'

Chabaud, the television man, wasn't at home. The Métro inspector hadn't returned from work, but his wife was there with a friend, sat in front of some petit fours and cups of hot chocolate.

'What do you want me to say? I don't even know who lives upstairs from us. If the man never left his apartment, then it's no surprise that I never bumped into him on the stairs. As for my husband, he has never been higher than this floor. What business would he have up there?'

Another woman in the apartment opposite, with a baby in a cradle, a little girl with a bare bottom and a sterilizer full of feeding bottles on the floor.

On the floor above, Miss Tuppler was tapping away on her typewriter. She was tall, sturdily built and, because of the heat, was wearing only pyjamas, her breasts showing through the half-open jacket. She felt no compulsion to button it up.

'A murder in the building? How exciting! Have you arrested the . . . how you say . . . murderer . . . And your name be Maigret? . . . Maigret from Quai des Orfèvres? . . .'

She moved towards the bottle of bourbon that was standing on a table.

'Do you drink?'

He did drink and listened to her gibberish for ten

minutes or so, wondering if she would ever cover up her breasts.

'The Clou Doré? . . . No . . . Never been . . . But in the States all the nightclubs are owned by gangsters . . . Was Palmari being a gangster?'

As Maigret moved from one floor to the next, it was as if he was passing through a sort of Paris in miniature, with the same contrasts as when you go from one neighbourhood or street to another.

The American woman lived in the midst of bohemian chaos. The apartment opposite was all soft furnishings, with an odour of sweets and jam. A white-haired man was sleeping in an armchair, a newspaper draped over his lap.

'Don't speak too loudly. He hates being woken up with a start. Are you collecting for charity?'

'No. I'm from the police.'

The old woman looked amazed.

'Really! The police! And this is such a quiet building! Don't tell me someone has been burgled.'

She smiled, and her face was as gentle and benign as that of a sister of Saint Vincent de Paul under her wimple.

'A serious crime? Is that why there were all these comings and goings this morning? No, inspector, I don't know anyone, except the concierge.'

The PE teacher on the third floor wasn't at home either, but a young woman with her eyes full of sleep opened the door, wrapped in a blanket.

'What? No. I don't know when he'll be back. I haven't been here before.'

'When did you meet him?'

'Yesterday evening, or rather this morning, as it was past midnight. In a bar on Rue de Presbourg. What's he done? He seemed like a decent guy to me.'

There was little point in pursuing this. She could barely speak, as she was nursing a massive hangover.

At the Massolettis, only the maid was in. She explained in very bad French that her mistress had gone to meet her husband at Fouquet's, and they were going to dine together in town.

Their apartment was more modern, lighter and brighter than the others in the building. There was a guitar lying on a sofa.

On Palmari's floor, Fernand Barillard hadn't come home yet. The door was answered by a very blonde, plump woman of about thirty, who was humming.

'Hey! I passed you on the stairs earlier. What are you selling?'

'Police Judiciaire.'

'Are you investigating what happened this morning?'

'How do you know something happened?'

'Your colleagues were making enough of a racket! I only had to open the door a little to hear their conversations. By the way, they have a funny way of talking about the dead, especially those who were cracking jokes as they carried the body downstairs.'

'Did you know Manuel Palmari?'

'I've never seen him but have sometimes heard him bellowing.'

'Bellowing? What do you mean?'

'He can't have been easy to live with. It's understandable, the concierge told me he was an invalid. But he used to get so angry! . . .'

'With Aline?'

'She's called Aline? A strange woman. At first, whenever I passed her on the stairs, I'd nod hello, but she would just look right through me. What sort of person is she? Were they married? Did she kill him?'

'What time does your husband go to work?'

'It depends. He doesn't keep fixed hours like an office worker.'

'Does he come home for lunch?'

'Rarely, as he is mostly working in another part of town or out in the suburbs. He is a commercial traveller.'

'I know. What time did he leave this morning?'

'I'm not sure, because I went out very early to do my shopping.'

'What do you mean by "very early"?'

'Around eight o'clock. When I got back, at nine thirty, he had gone.'

'Did you bump into your neighbour when you were out?'

'No. We probably don't shop in the same places.'

'Have you been married long?'

'Eight years.'

Dozens and dozens of questions, and just as many replies for Maigret to log in his memory. And from this pile, a few, maybe just one, would become significant at some point.

The barman was home, because he wasn't due to begin

work until six o'clock. The maid and the two children were in the first room, which had been transformed into a play room. A small child tugged on Maigret and shouted:

'Bang! Bang! You're dead.'

Tony Pasquier, whose hair was thick and coarse, was shaving himself for the second time that day. His wife was sewing a button back on to a pair of child's trousers.

'What name did you say? Palmari? Should I know him?'

'He's your downstairs neighbour, or rather he was, up until this morning, your downstairs neighbour.'

'Has something happened to him? I passed some policemen on the stairs and when I got back at two thirty my wife told me they had taken away a body.'

'Have you ever been to the Clou Doré?'

'Not personally, but I've sometimes sent customers there.'

'Why?'

'Some of them ask for decent places to eat in a particular neighbourhood. The Clou Doré has a good reputation. I used to know the maître d', Pernelle, who worked in Claridge's. He knows his stuff.'

'Don't you know who owns the place?'

'I've never bothered to find out.'

'And the woman, Aline Bauche, have you ever met her?'

'The girl with the dark hair and the tight dresses I've seen on the stairs?'

'She's your landlady.'

'That's news to me. I've never even spoken to her. What about you, Lulu?'

'I hate her type.'

'You see, Monsieur Maigret. Not much for you here. Maybe you'll have better luck another time.'

The Englishman wasn't at home. On the sixth floor, Maigret found a long corridor where the only illumination was from a skylight. On the courtyard side there was a huge attic where the tenants piled up their junk: old trunks, dressmakers' dummies, boxes and bits of flea market bric-à-brac.

On the front side of the building was a line of doors, like in a barracks. The door at the end was Yolande's, the maid of the tenants on the second floor. It was open, and he noticed a see-through nightdress lying on an unmade bed and sandals on the rug.

The next door, Amélia's according to the plan that Maigret had sketched in his notebook, was shut. So was the following one.

When he knocked on the fourth door, a weak voice told him to come in, and through all the birdcages that filled the room he could see a moon-faced old woman sitting in a Voltaire armchair next to the window.

He almost went out again, to leave her to her reverie. She was practically ageless, connected to this world only by a slender thread; she looked at the intruder with a serene smile.

'Come in, my dear sir. Don't be afraid of my birds.'

He hadn't been told that, apart from the canaries, she had a huge parrot, not caged but perched on a seesaw in the middle of the room. The bird started screeching:

'Polly! . . . Pretty Polly! . . . Are you hungry, Polly?'

He explained that he was from the police and that a crime had been committed in the building.

'I know, my dear sir. The concierge told me when I went to do my shopping. It's so sad that we kill each other when life is so short anyway! It's like in the wars. My father fought in 1870 and in 1914. I've lived through two wars myself.'

'Did you know Monsieur Palmari?'

'Neither him nor anyone else, apart from the concierge, who isn't as bad as you might think. The poor woman has had her problems in life. Her husband was a womanizer, and as if that wasn't bad enough, a drinker.'

'Have you ever heard any tenant come up to this floor?'

'Every now and again someone comes up to fetch something from the attic or put something away. But my window's always open, and my birds are always singing, so . . .'

'Do you see your next-door neighbour?'

'Monsieur Jef? You would think we were the same age. In fact, he is much younger than me. He can't be much more than seventy. He just seems older because of his wounds. Have you met him too? He is deaf and dumb, and I sometimes wonder if that isn't worse than being blind.

'People say the blind are happier folk than the deaf. I'll find out soon enough, as my eyesight is getting worse each day. I'd be unable to describe your face. I can only make out a light patch amid shadows. Won't you take a seat?'

Finally, the old man, who, when Maigret arrived, was reading a children's comic. His face was covered in scars, one of which ran upwards from the corner of his mouth, which made it look like he had a permanent smile on his face.

He wore tinted blue glasses. In the middle of the room a large white-wood table was covered in various odds and ends, unexpected objects, a small boy's Meccano set, pieces of carved wood, old magazines, a lump of clay that the old man had fashioned into some unidentifiable animal.

The iron bed looked like something in a barracks, as did the rough blanket, and on the whitewashed walls were hung posters representing sun-kissed cities: Nice, Naples, Istanbul . . . More magazines were piled up on the floor. With his hands, which weren't trembling, despite his age, the man tried to signal that he was deaf and dumb, that he couldn't speak, and Maigret responded with a gesture of helplessness. Then the man indicated that he could lip-read.

'Excuse me for disturbing you. I'm from the police. Did you by any chance know a tenant here called Palmari?'

Maigret pointed at the floor to indicate that Palmari lived down below, then raised two fingers to represent the number of floors. Old Jef shook his head, and Maigret asked him about Aline.

As far as he could gather, the old man had met her on the stairs. He described her in a somewhat droll manner, sculpting in thin air, as it were, the shape of her narrow face and her curvaceous, slim body.

When he got back to the fourth floor, Maigret felt as if he had visited a whole cross-section of humanity. He was more weighed down, a little sad. Manuel's death in his wheelchair had barely caused a ripple; there were people here who had lived just the width of a wall, ceiling or floor away from him for years and weren't even aware he had been carried away under a sheet.

Lucas wasn't playing cards. Aline wasn't in the living room.

'I think she's asleep.'

Young Lapointe was there, thrilled to be on duty with the chief.

'I took a car. Was that all right?'

'Any beer left, Lucas?'

'Two bottles.'

'Open one for me, and I'll have half a dozen delivered.'

It was six o'clock. The traffic jams were beginning to form across Paris, and a driver was beeping impatiently, contrary to regulations, beneath the windows of the apartment building.

4.

The Clou Doré on Rue Fontaine was flanked on one side by a third-rate strip club and on the other by a lingerie shop specializing in high-end women's underwear that foreigners took home with them as souvenirs of 'Gay Paree'.

Maigret and Lapointe had parked the police car on Rue Chaptal and were walking slowly up the street, where the people of the daytime were beginning to be supplanted by the altogether different-looking denizens of the night.

It was seven o'clock. The bouncer, whom everyone called Jo Muscles, wasn't yet at his post at the door of the restaurant, in his blue uniform with gold braid.

Maigret tried to locate him. He knew him well. He had the appearance of a former fairground boxer, though he had never actually pulled on boxing gloves. Aged around forty, he had spent half his life in the twilight, firstly as a minor in a reformatory, then in prison for spells of between six months and two years, for mindless thefts or for assault and battery.

He had the intelligence of a ten-year-old and when he encountered some unforeseen situation, he had a vague, almost pleading look in his eyes, like a schoolboy being tested by a teacher on a subject he hasn't swotted up on.

They would find him inside, in his livery, wiping down the tan leather banquettes with a cloth, and as soon as he spotted Maigret his face was as expressive as a wooden head.

The two waiters were busy laying the tables, setting out plates with the restaurant's crest on them, glasses and silver cutlery, as well as a centrepiece, a crystal flute containing a pair of flowers.

The lamps with pink shades weren't lit yet, as the pavement opposite was still bathed in golden sunlight.

The barman, Justin, in a white shirt and black tie, was giving the glasses a last quick wipe, and the only customer, a fat man with a red face, sat on a high stool drinking a crème de menthe.

Maigret had seen him somewhere. His face looked familiar, but he couldn't place him straight away. Had he come across him at the races, here even, or at his office in Quai des Orfèvres?

Montmartre was full of people he had had dealings with, sometimes many years earlier, who would disappear off the scene for a length of time, maybe for a stint in Fontevrault or Melun, or otherwise make themselves scarce until they had been forgotten about.

'Good evening, detective chief inspector. Good evening, inspector,' Justin said casually. 'If you're here for dinner you're a little early. What can I get you?'

'Beer.'

'Dutch, Danish, German?'

The manager emerged silently from the back room. He was almost bald, with a pale, somewhat puffy face and purple bags under his eyes.

Showing no surprise or obvious emotion, he came towards the policemen, offered Maigret a limp hand, then gripped Lapointe's, before leaning against the bar, without taking a seat. He had only his dinner jacket to put on before being ready to receive his customers.

'I was expecting to see you today. I'm even a bit surprised you didn't come earlier. What do you think of all this?'

He seemed tormented or in the grip of sadness.

'Think of all what?'

'Somebody got to him in the end. Do you have any idea who pulled the trigger?'

So, even though Manuel's death wasn't in the papers yet, even though Aline had remained under surveillance all day and hadn't made a single telephone call, the news had reached the Clou Doré.

If a policeman from the Ternes district had talked, it would have been to a reporter and in confidence. As for the tenants in the building, none of them seemed to have any connection with the Montmartre crowd.

'How long have you known, Jean-Loup?'

Jean-Loup was the first name of the manager, who also doubled as the maître d'. The police had nothing on him. Originally from the Allier, he had started out as a waiter in Vichy. He had married young and had children: his son was studying at medical school, and one of his daughters had married the owner of a restaurant on the Champs-Élysées. He led a respectable life in a villa he had had built in Choisy-le-Roi.

'I'm not sure,' he replied in surprise. 'Why do you ask me that? I thought everyone knew.'

'The papers haven't mentioned the crime. Try to remember. Did you already know at lunchtime?'

'I think so, yes. The customers talk to us about all sorts of things! Can you remember, Justin?'

'No. They were talking about it in the bar as well.'

'Who?'

Maigret was encountering the familiar code of silence. Even if Pernelle, the manager, wasn't part of their world and led the most orderly of lives, he was no less bound to secrecy by some of his customers.

The Clou Doré wasn't the bar of former times, when it was full of villains, and Palmari, who ran the place then, didn't need much persuading to give Maigret a tip-off.

The restaurant had acquired a wealthy clientele. It attracted a fair number of foreigners, some pretty girls too, around ten or eleven at night, because dinner was served until midnight. A few gang leaders had stuck to their old ways, but they were no longer youngsters up for anything. They all owned houses now, most of them had wives and children.

'I would like to know who first mentioned this to the pair of you.'

And Maigret went fishing, to employ his own expression.

'Could it have been a certain Massoletti?'

He had had time to memorize the names of all the tenants in the building on Rue des Acacias.

'What does he do?'

'Works in cars . . . Italian cars.'

'Don't know him. What about you, Justin?'

'First time I've heard the name.'

They both seemed to be telling the truth.

'Vignon?'

No hint of recognition in their eyes. They shook their heads.

'A PE teacher called Destouches?'

'Not known around here.'

'Tony Pasquier?'

'I know him,' broke in Justin.

'So do I,' added Pernelle. 'He sometimes sends me customers. He is second barman at Claridge's, isn't he? I haven't seen him for months.'

'Did he telephone today?'

'He only telephones when he wants to especially recommend a customer.'

'Was it maybe your bouncer who gave you the news?'

The latter, who had heard them speak, spat on the ground in a show of disgust and muttered between his dentures:

'It's a disgrace.'

'James Stuart, an Englishman? No? Fernand Barillard?'

With each name the two men seemed to be racking their brains before shaking their heads again.

'Who do you think might have had an interest in getting rid of Palmari?'

'It's not the first time someone's had a go.'

'Except that the two men who sprayed him with machine guns were bumped off themselves. And Palmari never left his apartment again. Tell me, Pernelle. How long ago was it that the Clou Doré changed hands?'

A slight blush on the manager's pale face.

'Five days.'

'And who is the current owner?'

He hesitated just for a moment. He realized that Maigret was in the know and that it would be pointless to lie.

'Me.'

'Who did you buy the place from?'

'From Aline, of course.'

'How long had Aline been the real owner?'

'I can't remember the date. More than two years.'

'Was the sale handled by a lawyer?'

'It was all completely above board.'

'Who was the lawyer?'

'Maître Desgrières, Boulevard Pereire.'

'The price?'

'Two hundred grand.'

'New francs, I take it?'

'Of course.'

'Paid in cash?'

'Yes, even though it took ages to count all the notes.'

'Did Aline take them away in a bag or a briefcase?'

'I don't know. I left first.'

'Did you know that the building on Rue des Acacias was also owned by the late Manuel's mistress?'

The two men were feeling more and more ill at ease.

'There are always rumours going round. Listen, inspector, I'm an honest man, and so is Justin. We both have families. Because the restaurant is in Montmartre we have all sorts among our clientele. By law, we're not allowed to kick them out unless they are blind drunk, which is rarely the case.

'We hear rumours, but we prefer to forget them. Isn't that so, Justin?'

'Exactly.'

'I wonder,' Maigret murmured, 'whether Aline had a lover.'

Neither of them flinched, neither said yes or no, which surprised Maigret somewhat.

'Did she ever meet men here?'

'She didn't even stop at the bar. She came straight to my office on the mezzanine, went through the accounts like a businesswoman, then took the money that was owing to her.'

'Don't you find it strange that a man like Palmari had, so it seems, transferred all, or at least a good part, of what he owned to her name?'

'Lots of tradesmen and businessmen sign over their property to their wives if they are worried it might be repossessed.'

'Palmari wasn't married,' Maigret pointed out. 'And there were thirty-five years between them.'

'That crossed my mind too. Look, I think Manuel was really crazy about Aline. He had complete faith in her. He loved her. I'd swear he'd never really been in love before he met her. He felt diminished in his invalid's wheelchair. More than ever, she became his life, the only being who connected him to the outside world.'

'What about her?'

'As far as I can tell, she loved him. It happens to girls like her too. Before she knew him she had only ever come across men who used her for their pleasure without seeing her as a human being, do you understand? The Alines of this world are more susceptible than respectable women to the attention you show them, to affection and to a life of security.'

The fat, ruddy man at the other end of the bar ordered another crème de menthe.

'Coming right up, Monsieur Louis.'

Maigret whispered:

'Who is this Monsieur Louis?'

'A customer. I don't know his surname, but he comes in here quite often to drink a menthe or two with water. I presume he must live around here.'

'Was he in here for an aperitif before lunch?'

'Was he here, Justin?' Pernelle repeated quietly.

'Hold on. I think so. He asked me if I had a tip for a race – can't remember which one.'

Monsieur Louis mopped his brow as he stared mournfully at his glass.

Maigret took his notebook out of his pocket, wrote a few words and showed them to Lapointe:

If he goes out, follow him. Meet me back here. If I'm gone, phone me at home.

'Since you aren't too busy yet, Pernelle, would it bother you if we went up to the mezzanine for a while?'

It was an invitation that a restaurant owner can hardly refuse.

'This way . . .'

He had flat feet and waddled like a duck, like most

78

maître d's of a certain age. The staircase was narrow and dark. Up here, there was none of the luxury and comfort of the restaurant. Pernelle pulled a bunch of keys from his pocket, opened a door that had been painted brown, and they found themselves in a small room overlooking the courtyard.

The roll-top desk was covered in bills, brochures, two telephones, pens, pencils and letterheaded documents. On the white-wood shelves were rows of green filing cases, and on the opposite wall there were framed photographs of Madame Pernelle looking twenty or thirty years younger, of a young man of about twenty and a young girl leaning forward pensively, her chin resting in her hand.

'Sit down, Pernelle, and listen to me. Shall we be straight with one another?'

'I've always been straight.'

'You know that's not true, that you can't allow yourself to be, otherwise you wouldn't be the owner of the Clou Doré. To put you at your ease I will tell you something that is now no longer of consequence for the person concerned.

'When Manuel bought what was then just a bistro, twenty years ago, I used to pop in for a drink in the morning, at a time when I was fairly sure of finding him alone.

'He would also phone me or pay discreet visits to Quai des Orfèvres.'

'An informer?' murmured Pernelle without a great deal of surprise.

'Did you suspect him?'

'I'm not sure. Maybe. I guess that's why they shot him three years ago?'

'Possibly. Only, Manuel was smart, and if he occasionally fed me information on some small fry, he was also involved in serious stuff that he was very careful not to breathe a word about.'

'Do you want me to have a bottle of champagne brought up?'

'It's more or less the only drink that doesn't tempt me.'

'Beer?'

'Not right now.'

Pernelle was clearly uncomfortable.

'Manuel was very clever,' Maigret continued, still holding the other man's gaze. 'So clever we could never find anything on him. He knew that I knew at least a good part of the truth. He didn't bother to deny it. He would look at me calmly, with a hint of irony, and when it was necessary he would surrender up one of his confederates.'

'I don't understand.'

'Yes you do.'

'What do you mean by that? I've never worked for Manuel, except here, as his maître d', then as his manager.'

'Nevertheless, by lunchtime today you already knew what had happened to him. As you said, you hear a lot of things at the bar or in the restaurant. What do you think about the jewellery thefts, Pernelle?'

'What they say in the newspapers: amateurs trying it on, who will all get caught in the end.'

'No.'

'They say that there is this old guy who always hangs around nearby to guard against all eventualities.'

'What else?'

'Nothing. I swear to you that I don't know anything else.'

'All right! I'll elaborate, in the knowledge that I'm not telling you anything you don't know already. What is the biggest risk run by jewel thieves?'

'Getting caught?'

'When?'

'When they sell the jewels.'

'Good. We're getting somewhere. All stones of a certain value have an ID, as it were, and are well known to people in the trade. Whenever there is a theft, a description of the jewels is circulated, not just in France, but abroad.

'A receiver, if the thieves know one, will only pay around ten or fifteen per cent of the value of the haul. Almost always, when he puts the stones back in circulation, a year or two later, the police will identify them and trace them back to their source. Agreed?'

'I assume that's how it works. You know more about these things than I do.'

'Now, for years, jewels have regularly been going missing following some hold-up or smash-and-grab and disappearing without trace. What does that imply?'

'Search me.'

'Come on, Pernelle. You don't do your trade for thirty or forty years without knowing the ropes, even if you aren't directly involved.'

'I haven't been in Montmartre long.'

'The first task is not only to remove the diamonds from their settings, but also to transform them, which requires the assistance of a diamond cutter. Do you know any?'

'No.'

'Few people do, for the good reason that there aren't that many of them, not just in France, but in the world as a whole. There are no more than about fifteen of them in Paris, largely grouped in the Marais, in the streets around Rue des Francs-Bourgeois, and they are a tightly knit community. Besides, the brokers, the diamond dealers and the big jewellers who give them work all have their eye on them.'

'I hadn't thought of that.'

'You don't say!'

There was a knock at the door. It was the barman, who handed Maigret a slip of paper.

'Someone just brought this for you.'

'Who?'

'The waiter from the tabac on the corner.'

Lapointe had scribbled in pencil on a page from a notebook:

He went into the phone booth to make a call. Through the glass, I could see that he was asking for Étoile 42.39. Not sure about the last digit. He sat down in a corner and read a newspaper. I'm still here.

'Would you allow me to use one of your phones? By the way, why do you have two lines?'

'I only have one. The second phone is just connected to the restaurant.'

'Hello? Directory Inquiries? Detective Chief Inspector Maigret from the Police Judiciaire. I would like to know as quickly as possible which subscriber has the number Étoile 42.39. Some doubt over the last digit. Would you be so kind as to ring me back on this number?'

'Right,' he said to Pernelle, 'I wouldn't mind that glass of beer.'

'Are you sure you don't know more than you have told me about Monsieur Louis?'

Pernelle hesitated, realizing that he was in deep water now.

'I don't know him personally. I see him at the bar. I sometimes serve him when Justin isn't there, and we've chatted about the weather.'

'Is there ever anyone with him?'

'Rarely. I've seen him with young guys once or twice and wondered if he was queer.'

'Do you know his surname or his address?'

'I've only ever heard him referred to as Monsieur Louis, and always with a certain respect. He must live in the neighbourhood, as he never comes by car.'

The telephone rang. Maigret picked up.

'Inspector Maigret? I think I have the information that you were looking for,' said the Directory Inquiries operator. 'Étoile 42.39 suspended his subscription six months ago when he went abroad. The subscriber to Étoile 42.38 is called Fernand Barillard and he lives . . .'

Maigret knew the rest. The luxury packaging salesman who lived on the same floor as Palmari!

'Thank you, mademoiselle.'

'Don't you want the preceding numbers?'

'Why not? Just in case . . .'

The other names and addresses were unknown to him. Maigret hauled himself to his feet, dazed by the heat and a tiring day.

'Think about what I said, Pernelle. Now you're your own boss and own a successful restaurant, it would be a shame to have problems to deal with, wouldn't it? I have an idea I'll be seeing you again before too long. A word of advice: don't speak too much about the conversation we've just had, either on the telephone or otherwise. By the way, does luxury packaging ring any bells with you?'

The new owner of the Clou Doré looked at him with genuine surprise.

'I don't follow.'

'Some packagers specialize in chocolate boxes, sweet cones, etcetera. And among this etcetera might be included boxes used by jewellers instead of proper cases.'

He went down the dark and dirty staircase and crossed the restaurant, where there were now a couple sitting in the corner and four slightly inebriated diners around a table.

He went back up the street to the bar-tabac, spotted Lapointe sitting abstemiously in front of an aperitif and, in the corner, Monsieur Louis, who was reading the evening paper. Neither of them saw him, and a few moments later, Maigret was climbing into a taxi.

'Rue des Acacias, on the corner of Rue de l'Arc-de-Triomphe.'

The sky was turning a flaming red, colouring the faces

of the passers-by. There wasn't a breath of wind, and Maigret could feel his shirt sticking to his body. During the journey, he seemed to doze, and perhaps actually did doze off, since the driver gave him a start when he said:

'We're here, boss.'

He raised his head and looked from top to bottom at the light-brick building with white-stone window surrounds, which must have been built around 1910. The lift took him to the fourth floor, and he almost, out of habit, rang the doorbell to the left.

Outside the door to the right he was left waiting for a while, until the blonde woman he had questioned that afternoon opened to him, with her mouth full and a hand holding a napkin.

'You again!' she said, not bad-temperedly, but with surprise. 'My husband and I are having dinner.'

'I'd like to have a few words with him.'

'Come in.'

The living room resembled the one opposite, though it was less luxurious and had a cheaper carpet. They then entered not a little room as at Palmari's, but a bourgeois dining room with rustic furniture.

'It's Inspector Maigret, Fernand.'

A man of about forty, his face bisected by a dark moustache, stood up, he too with a napkin in his hand. He had taken off his jacket, unknotted his tie and opened the collar of his shirt.

'I'm honoured,' he murmured, looking at his wife and the visitor in turn.

'The inspector has already been this afternoon. I didn't

have time to tell you. Because of the tenant who died he has been going round the building, ringing at all the doors.'

'Please, carry on with your meal,' said Maigret. 'I have plenty of time.'

On the table there was some roast veal and noodles in tomato sauce. The couple returned to their seats, feeling somewhat embarrassed while the inspector sat down at the end of the table.

'Would you like a glass of wine?'

There was a carafe of white wine fresh from the refrigerator and misty with condensation; Maigret couldn't resist. He was right not to, for it was a local wine from Sancerre, dry and fruity at the same time, which surely hadn't been bought from a corner grocery shop.

There was an awkward silence as the Barillards resumed eating with their guest observing them vaguely.

'All I could tell him was that we didn't know Palmari. For my part, I've never seen him and until this morning I didn't even know his name. As for his wife . . .'

Her husband was a good-looking man, slim and well built, who was no doubt popular with women, and his moustache accentuated his full lips and his perfect teeth, which were revealed whenever he smiled.

'Do you know them?'

'No. But let the inspector speak. I'm listening, Monsieur Maigret.'

There was a hint of irony about him, and aggression lurking just under the surface. He was a handsome male, very self-confident, up for a fight, sure of both his charm and his strength.

'Finish your meal first. Did you have a lot of calls to make today?'

'I was in the Lilas district.'

'In a car?'

'In my car, yes, of course. I have a Peugeot 404, which suits me fine and which looks the part. In my line of work, these things matter.'

'I suppose you carry a case full of samples?'

'Like all my colleagues.'

'When you have eaten your fruit, I will ask you to show it to me.'

'That's an odd thing to be interested in, isn't it?'

'It all depends on your point of view.'

'May I ask you if you have made requests of a similar nature on the other floors of the building?'

'Not yet, Monsieur Barillard. I should add that you have the right to refuse, in which case I will telephone a very helpful examining magistrate, who will send an orderly with a search warrant and, if necessary, an arrest warrant. Perhaps you would rather we carried on this conversation in my office at Quai des Orfèvres?'

Maigret couldn't fail to notice the contrasting reactions of the couple. The woman was wide-eyed, surprised by the unexpected turn the conversation had taken and the way the two men were squaring up to each other.

Placing her hand on her husband's, she asked:

'What's going on, Fernand?'

'Nothing, darling. Don't worry. Shortly, Inspector Maigret will be apologizing to me. When the police find themselves at a loss with a crime, they tend to go on wild goose chases.'

'Madame, did you receive a telephone call a little less than an hour ago?'

She glanced at her husband as if asking him how she should reply, but he didn't look at her. Instead, he seemed to be sizing up Maigret, trying to guess where he was going with this.

'I took the phone call.'

'Was it a friend?'

'A client.'

'A chocolate-maker? Confectioner? Perfumer? That's your clientele, isn't it?'

'You're well informed.'

'Unless it was a jeweller? May I ask you to tell me his name, Monsieur Barillard?'

'I confess I didn't make a note of it, because his business wasn't of interest to me.'

'Really! A client who rings you after work. What did he want from you?'

'Our current prices.'

'Have you known Monsieur Louis long?'

That struck home. Handsome Fernand frowned, and his wife noticed he looked suddenly ill at ease.

'I don't know Monsieur Louis. Now, if you feel it is necessary to continue this conversation, let us go to my study. I'm not in favour of bringing women into business matters, on principle.'

'Women?'

'My wife, if you prefer. Will you excuse us, dear?'

He led Maigret into an adjoining room, with the same dimensions, more or less, as Palmari's little room and quite comfortably furnished. As the windows looked out on to the courtyard, it was darker than the other rooms, and Barillard turned on the lamps.

'Take a seat, if you wish. Since I have no choice, I will listen to what you have to say.'

'You just said something amusing.'

'I can assure you I have no intention to amuse you. We had plans to go to the cinema this evening, my wife and I, and you will make us miss the start of the film. So what did I say that was so funny?'

'That on principle you didn't like to involve women in business matters.'

'I'm not unusual in that.'

'We'll come back to that later. As far as Madame Barillard is concerned, at least, I'm inclined to believe you. Have you been married long?'

'Eight years.'

'Were you in the same line of business as you are now?'

'Pretty much the same, yes.'

'What was different?'

'I was more on the production side, in a cardboard factory in Fontenay-sous-Bois.'

'Were you living in this building?'

'No, in a house in Fontenay.'

'Let's take a look at your case of samples.'

It was lying on the floor to the left of the door, and Barillard reluctantly hoisted it on to his desk.

'The key?'

'It's not locked.'

Maigret opened it and, as he expected, among the luxury boxes, almost all of them tastefully decorated, he found some of those boxes that jewellers use for watches and jewels that are sold without cases.

'How many jewellers have you visited today?'

'I don't know. Three or four. Clockmakers and jewellers are just a small part of our clientele.'

'Do you keep a note of the establishments you visit?'

Once again, Fernand Barillard twitched.

'I don't have the mentality of an accountant or a statistician. I simply write down the orders.'

'And of course, when you pass on the orders to your firm, you keep copies?'

'Maybe others do that. I have complete faith in my employers and I weigh myself down as little as possible with paperwork.'

'So you wouldn't be able to provide me with a list of your customers?'

'That's right, I wouldn't.'

'What is the name of your company?'

'Gelot and Son, Avenue des Gobelins.'

'I'm sure they keep better records than you do, and I will visit them in the morning.'

'Can you tell me what you are hoping to achieve?'

'A question for you, first. You claim that you never mix women and business, correct?'

Barillard lit a cigarette and shrugged his shoulders.

'But what if that woman is called Aline and lives on your doorstep?'

'I didn't know she was called Aline.'

'But you knew straight away who I was talking about.'

'There is only one other apartment on this floor, hence "on our doorstep", and, as far as I know, only one woman in that apartment.

'I've sometimes crossed her on the stairs or shared the lift with her and tipped my hat in greeting, but I don't recall ever having spoken to her.

'Maybe I might have just sometimes held open the door of the lift and murmured: "After you." '

'Does your wife know?'

'Know about what?'

'Everything. Your work. Your various activities. Your relationship with Monsieur Louis.'

'I told you that I don't know Monsieur Louis.'

'Yet an hour ago he telephoned to warn you that I was making inquiries on Rue Fontaine and he reported part of my conversation with the owner of the Clou Doré and his barman.'

'What do you want me to say?'

'Nothing. As you see, I'm doing the talking. Sometimes it's best to be up front, lay all your cards on the table.

'I could have waited until I'd seen your employers and questioned the accountant at Avenue des Gobelins. They wouldn't have had time to fiddle the books to cover your back. And you know very well what I will find there.'

'Names, addresses and figures. Lots of Pompadour boxes at a hundred and fifty francs a dozen. Lots of—'

'Lots of jewel boxes at so much a dozen or a hundred.'

'So what?'

'Consider, Monsieur Barillard, that I have in my possession a list of jewellers in Paris and in the suburbs which have been the targets of major thefts in the last few years, whether hold-ups or, more recently, smash-and-grabs using tyre levers to break the window.

'Do you see what I'm getting at? I am as good as certain that on the list of your clients that Gelot and Son will provide me I will find more or less all the names I have on my own list.'

'So what if you do? Given that I visit most of the jewellers in the area, except the large firms that use only fine leather cases, you'd expect—'

'I don't think the examining magistrate in charge of the Palmari case will be of the same opinion.'

'Because my neighbour is in the jewel trade too?'

'In a manner of speaking. And for the last three years, since he has been an invalid, with the help of a woman.'

'Is that why you asked me earlier whether—'

'Exactly. Now, I am asking you if you are Aline Bauche's lover and for how long.'

It was an instinctive reaction. In spite of himself, the man cast a furtive glance at the door, then tiptoed across and opened it to make sure his wife wasn't listening there.

'If you had talked to me like this in the dining room I'd have punched your lights out. You can't just come into my house and cast suspicion in this way.'

'You didn't answer my question.'

'The answer's no.'

'And you still claim you don't know Monsieur Louis?'

'I don't know Monsieur Louis.'

'May I?'

Maigret reached out for the telephone, dialled the number of the apartment opposite and recognized Lucas' voice.

'What is your client doing?'

'She slept for a while, then she ate a slice of ham and an egg. She is getting agitated and has started pacing round the apartment, looking daggers at me every time she walks past me.'

'Has she tried to make a phone call?'

'No. I'm keeping a close eye on her.'

'Any visitors?'

'No, no one.'

'Thank you. I'll be there in a few minutes. In the meantime, can you ring headquarters and get them to send another man? Here, yes. I know Bonfils is downstairs.

'I want a second man, and you will give him the following instruction: first, he should pick up a car; second, he should park outside the main door and never let it out of his sight.

'His job is to tail a certain Fernand Barillard, if he emerges either alone or with his wife. He is the travelling salesman who lives in the apartment opposite the one you are in now.

'I'm here now, yes. Have someone put a tap on his line.

'Description of Barillard: about forty, one metre seventy-five, thick dark hair, slim dark moustache, elegantly dressed, a ladies' man. His wife, if she happens to be with him, is about ten years younger, blonde, attractive, fairly plump.

'I'll stay here until the new inspector arrives. See you later, then.'

While he was speaking, Barillard was giving him a hateful stare.

'I assume,' said Maigret in an almost bland tone, 'that you still have nothing to say to me?'

'Absolutely nothing.'

'It will take about ten minutes for my inspector to get here. I intend to keep you company until then.'

'As you wish.'

Barillard sat down in a leather chair, picked up a magazine from a side-table and pretended to be absorbed in an article. Maigret stood up and started examining the room in detail, reading the titles of books on the bookshelves, lifting up a paperweight, opening desk drawers.

For Barillard these were ten long minutes. He would occasionally glance over the top of his magazine at this thick-set, placid man who seemed to fill the study with his bulk, to crush it under his weight, and whose expression was completely unreadable.

From time to time, Maigret took his watch from his pocket, for he had never got used to wristwatches and treasured the double-case golden fob watch he had inherited from his father.

'Four more minutes, Monsieur Barillard.'

Barillard tried not to flinch, but his hands gave away his impatience.

'Three minutes.'

He restrained himself, but only with the greatest difficulty.

'There we are! I wish you goodnight and look forward to our next interview, which I hope will be just as cordial as this one.'

Maigret left the study and found the young woman, her eyes red, in the dining room.

'My husband hasn't done anything wrong, has he, inspector?'

'You'll have to ask him, madame. I hope not, for your sake.'

'Despite appearances, he is a very gentle, affectionate man. He's a bit short-tempered sometimes, but that's just his nature, and he's always the first to be sorry afterwards.'

'Goodnight, madame.'

She saw him out with a worried look in her eyes and watched as he headed not for the lift but for the door opposite.

5.

When Aline opened the door to him, she looked worried; she gazed at him intensely, dark rings under her eyes. Maigret was more placid than ever. In the time it took to cross the landing, he had adopted that easy-going demeanour that his inspectors knew well and were never taken in by.

'I didn't want to leave the building without wishing you as good a night as possible.'

Lucas, who was sitting in an armchair, put the magazine he was reading on the carpet and stood up lazily. It was quite evident that the atmosphere between these two people who had just spent several hours together in the apartment and were destined to spend several more before morning was far from cordial.

'Don't you think you'd be better off going to bed, Aline? It's been an emotionally draining day. I fear that tomorrow will be just as difficult, if not more so. Do you have some sort of sleeping pill or tranquillizer in your medicine cabinet?'

She gave him a hard stare, trying to read his innermost thoughts, furious that the inspector was giving her no way in.

'For my part, I learned a lot this morning, but I need to verify certain things before I talk to you about what I have discovered. Only this evening, in fact, I made the acquaint-ance of the rather curious fellow who lives across the landing from you.

'I was wrong about him at first and assumed he was merely a salesman working in chocolate and sweet boxes.

'It turns out his business is more wide-ranging and incorporates in particular the world of jewellery.'

He took his time, refilled his pipe, apparently miles away.

'With all this going on, I haven't had dinner yet. I hope Monsieur Louis will still be there waiting for me at the Clou Doré and that we can eat together.'

Another silence. He pushed down the tobacco with a familiar prod of his index finger, picked out a stray flake, then finally struck a match, while Aline watched these painstaking movements with growing impatience.

'A handsome man, that Fernand Barillard. I wouldn't have thought one woman would be enough for him, espe-cially as his wife seems a tad insipid for the likes of him. What do you think?'

'I don't know him.'

'Naturally, the landlady of a building can't know all her tenants intimately. Especially since I ask myself whether this is the only property you own.

'I'll find out tomorrow, from Maître Desgrières, with whom I have an appointment. This is a complicated busi-ness, Aline, and I don't always feel I have a firm footing in it.

'To be on the safe side, I've posted a man downstairs, in case Barillard feels a need to go out. And his telephone line, like yours, has been tapped.

'So, you see, I've given you fair warning. No doubt you have nothing to say to me?'

Tight-lipped, she strode off with clipped, robotic steps to her bedroom and slammed the door behind her.

'Is it true, chief, all that stuff you just said?'

'Most of it. Goodnight. Try to stay awake. Make yourself as much strong coffee as you need and if anything happens ring me at Boulevard Richard-Lenoir. I don't know what time I'll be there, but I'm determined to get some sleep.'

Rather than take the lift, he slowly walked down the stairs, imagining the lives of each of the tenants as he passed their door. Some of them were watching television, and the same voices and the same music could be heard coming out of several different apartments. In Mabel Tuppler's, heavy footsteps suggested one or two couples dancing. Inspector Lagrune was dozing at the wheel of a police car, and Maigret shook his hand distractedly.

'Don't you have a car, chief?'

'I'll find a taxi on Avenue de la Grande-Armée. Do you have your instructions?'

'Follow that man, Fernand Barillard.'

Maigret felt less light at heart than when he had woken up that morning with sunlight streaming into his apartment, or when he had stood on the bus platform soaking up images of Paris coloured like in a children's album.

People were often very keen to ask him about his methods. Some even thought they could analyse them, and he would look at them with mocking curiosity, since they obviously knew more about them than he did: more often than not, he simply followed his gut instincts and improvised.

The prefect would certainly not have appreciated what Maigret's gut instincts were telling him that day, and the little examining magistrate, in spite of his admiration for Maigret, would probably have frowned.

For example, before questioning Fernand Barillard, Maigret should have collected as much information as possible about his subject, built up a case, already have at his fingertips the dates he was so sure of finding at Gelot and Son, the exact details that Maître Desgrières would possibly provide him with.

He had chosen instead to sow anxiety in Barillard's mind, deliberately to put him on his guard, not hide the fact – indeed, quite the contrary – that he was under surveillance.

Momentarily, he had considered not saying anything at all to Aline and instead surprising her the next day by putting her in the same room as her next-door neighbour and observing their reactions.

In the end, he had played the opposite game, and now she knew that he had established a link between her and the cardboard-box salesman.

They were both under surveillance. They could neither meet nor make contact by telephone. They couldn't leave the building without being followed.

Would they get a good night's sleep under those circumstances? Maigret had done the same thing with Monsieur Louis, making it clear that his every move would now be recorded by the police.

He was still unable to establish the links between these three individuals. The only thing they had in common was their discomfort, which Maigret did his best to make as acute as possible for all three of them.

'Take me to the Clou Doré, Rue Fontaine.'

There, too, he had effectively laid his cards on the table. And since he had to eat somewhere, he might as well do so at the restaurant of which Palmari was for a long time the owner, before putting it in Aline's name, then selling it to Pernelle.

He was surprised when he walked in to find such a lively atmosphere. Almost all the tables were occupied, and there was a babble of conversation interspersed with women's laughter, while the cigar and cigarette smoke formed an almost opaque cloud a metre from the ceiling.

In the pink glow of the lamps, he noticed Monsieur Louis at a table opposite a pretty girl, while Lapointe was cooling his heels at the bar and nursing a bitter lemon.

Pernelle had his professional smile plastered on and was circulating among the customers, shaking hands, leaning over to hear a good story, or to take an order, which he then passed on to one of the waiters.

Two women, perched on stools at the bar, were trying to catch the eye of young Lapointe, who seemed embarrassed and was trying to look the other way.

When Maigret arrived, one of them turned to her companion, no doubt to whisper:

'He's a cop!'

So when Maigret walked over to talk to Lapointe, the two ladies suddenly lost interest in the young man.

'Have you had dinner?'

'I had a sandwich in the café-tabac when he stopped off there for an hour. Afterwards, he came here and waited for this young woman before they took a table.'

'Not too tired?'

'I'm fine.'

'I'd like you to carry on following him. When he goes home, telephone headquarters and ask for someone to relieve you. Same thing if he goes to the girl's place, which is possible, or they go to a hotel. You'd better grab a bite with me.'

'A beer, Monsieur Maigret?'

'It's a bit late, Justin. I've had my fill of beer for today.'

He signalled to Pernelle, who found them a small table illuminated by a golden lamp with a silk shade.

'This evening I recommend the paella. You might have ramequins à la niçoise as starter. A nice dry Tavel to go with that, unless you prefer a Pouilly-Fumé.'

'The paella and the Tavel.'

'For two?'

He nodded and during the meal he seemed to be interested only in the food and the delightfully fruity wine. For his part, Monsieur Louis pretended to have eyes only for his companion, who nonetheless turned round at least two or three times to look at the policemen and no doubt asked questions about them.

'The more I see him,' Maigret sighed, 'the more I think I've come across him somewhere before. A long time ago, maybe ten years ago or more. It's possible I had dealings with him when he was young and thin, and his extra weight is confusing me.'

When the bill came, Pernelle leaned over in a professional manner and found the time to whisper in Maigret's ear:

'I remembered one thing after you left. There was a rumour going round a while back that Palmari owned a hotel on Rue de l'Étoile. It was a sleazy joint, Hôtel Bussière or Bessière.'

Maigret paid without seeming to attach much importance to this information.

'I'm going to check it out, Lapointe,' he murmured a while later. 'I don't expect I'll be there long. Good luck.'

Monsieur Louis watched him walk to the door. A taxi was passing. Ten minutes later, Maigret got out of the car opposite the Hôtel Bussière, situated less than 100 metres from the police station, which didn't stop two or three girls lingering there with obvious intent.

'You coming?'

He shook his head and found a night clerk behind the counter that separated the corridor from a small room in which could be seen a roll-top desk, a key rack and a camp bed.

'Is it for one night? Are you alone? Do you have any bags? In that case I have to ask you to pay in advance. Thirty francs, plus twenty per cent service charge.'

He pushed a register under Maigret's nose.

'Name, address, passport or identity card number.'

If Maigret had had a girl with him he would have bypassed these formalities.

After the trap that had been laid for him two weeks earlier and had almost forced him into retirement, he preferred not to compromise himself.

He wrote down his name, his address and card number, omitting his profession. He was given a key, and the ill-shaven clerk pushed an electric button which rang on the floor above.

It wasn't a chambermaid but a man in shirt-sleeves and a white apron who met him on the first floor and took his key, looking at the number on it with a surly expression.

'Forty-two? Follow me.'

The hotel didn't have a lift, which explained the porter's bad mood. The night staff at these second- or third-rate hotels is often made up of the dregs of humanity, and there are enough of them to fill an entire slum.

This particular porter had a limp, a crooked nose and a yellow pallor that suggested his liver was shot.

'Stairs and more stairs!' he muttered to himself. 'Bloody hell.'

On the fourth floor he led the way down a narrow corridor and stopped outside number 42.

'Here you are. I'll bring you some towels.'

Because there were no towels in the rooms: a classic trick to get a tip on top of the twenty per cent service charge.

The porter then made a show of checking that nothing was missing, and then his eye was caught by the fifty-franc note that Maigret was ostentatiously holding between two fingers.

'Is that for me?'

He grew suspicious but couldn't prevent his eyes lighting up.

'Looking for a pretty girl? Didn't find what you are after downstairs?'

'Close the door for a moment.'

'Hey, you don't have anything in mind, do you? It's funny, I feel like I know your face.'

'Maybe I remind you of someone. Do you always work at night?'

'Not me. I do the night shift every other week when I have to go into hospital for treatment.'

'So you sometimes work in the daytime and know some of the regular customers?'

'I know some of them. Others are just passing through.'

His red-rimmed eyes drifted from the banknote to the inspector's face, and his forehead creased, displaying a painful attempt to think.

'Can you tell me if you know this woman?'

Maigret pulled from his pocket a picture of Aline Bauche he had taken without her knowledge several months earlier.

'I'd like to know if she ever comes here accompanied by a man.'

The porter merely glanced at the photo, and his brow darkened even more.

'Are you making fun of me?'

'Why?'

'Because this is a picture of the owner. At least, as far as I know.'

'Do you see her often?'

'Not at night, at any rate. I sometimes see her when I'm on days.'

'Does she have a room at the hotel?'

'A suite, on the first floor.'

'But she isn't there regularly?'

'Like I said, I don't know. Sometimes we see her, sometimes we don't. It isn't any of our business and we're not paid to stick our noses in.'

'Do you know where she lives?'

'How would I?'

'Or her name?'

'I've heard the manageress call her Madame Bauche.'

'When she comes to the hotel, does she stay long?'

'It's impossible to say, because there's a spiral staircase that links the manageress's office on the ground floor with the apartment on the first.'

'Can you also get to the apartment using the main stairs?'

'Of course.'

'Take this money. It's yours.'

'Are you from the police?'

'Maybe.'

'Hold on, you aren't Inspector Maigret by any chance, are you? I thought your face was familiar. I hope you aren't going to cause the owner any trouble, because then I'll be in it too.'

'I promise to keep you out of it.'

A second banknote appeared as if by magic in Maigret's hand.

'In return for an honest answer to a simple question.'

'Let's hear the question first.'

'When she comes to the hotel, does Madame Bauche, as you call her, meet anyone other than the manageress?'

'She doesn't deal with the staff, if that's what you're driving at.'

'That's not what I mean. She might receive visitors from outside, who might not use the spiral staircase but will come up the main stairs . . .'

The second banknote was as enticing as the first. Maigret cut through the man's hesitation with a direct question:

'What is he like?'

'I've only seen him a couple of times, almost always in the afternoon. He's younger, slimmer than you.'

'Dark hair? Thin dark moustache? Handsome?'

The porter nodded.

'Was he carrying a case?'

'Mostly, yes. He rents a room on the first floor, always the same one, number seven, the one nearest the apartment, and he never spends the night there.'

The banknote changed hands, and the porter slipped it quickly into his pocket, but he didn't leave straight away, just in case there was a third question that might earn him another fifty francs.

'Thank you. I promise you won't be involved. I'll be leaving in a few minutes.'

When the bell went again, the porter dashed out of the room, calling out:

'I'm coming!'

'You didn't get too hot, did you?' Madame Maigret asked worriedly. 'I hope you took enough time to have lunch and dinner and didn't just make do with sandwiches.'

'I had an excellent paella at the Clou Doré. And for lunch, I can't remember. Oh yes, I ate with a funny little examining magistrate in an Auvergnat bistro.'

He had trouble getting to sleep, because all the people he had encountered that day came back to haunt him, one after the other, primarily the strangely twisted, almost grotesque form of Palmari lying in front of his wheelchair.

For Ancelin, he was simply a victim in a case that would occupy his attention only for a few weeks. Maigret, however, had known Manuel at different stages of his career; even though they were on different sides of the fence, the two men had forged subtle, almost indefinable bonds between them.

Could it be said that the inspector respected the former owner of the Clou Doré? That would be overstating it. Leaving aside all preconceptions, the senior policeman could not help holding the man in some esteem.

In the same way, he had from the start been curious about Aline, who exerted a certain fascination on him. He tried hard to understand her and sometimes thought he had, only then to call his judgement into question.

Finally, he slipped into the floating zone between waking and sleep, and the figures started to blur, and his thoughts became hazy and vague.

Fundamentally, there is fear. He had often talked about this when he was awake, with Doctor Pardon, who, like him, had a lot of experience of people and had come to very similar conclusions.

Everyone is afraid. We help young children overcome their fears with fairy tales, and then as soon as they get to school they are scared of showing their parents a school report with bad marks in it.

Fear of water. Fear of fire. Fear of animals, fear of the

dark. Fear, at the age of fifteen or sixteen, of making wrong choices and ruining your life.

In a state of semi-consciousness, all these fears became like the notes of a muted, tragic symphony: the hidden fears we drag behind us right through to the end, the acute fears that make us scream, the fears we make light of after the event, the fear of an accident, of illness, of the policeman, the fear of other people, of what they might say or think, of the way they look at you as they walk past.

Earlier, when he had stared at the banknote between Maigret's fingers, the sickly porter at the Hôtel Bussière was torn between the fear of losing his job and temptation. Then, with every banknote dangled before him, the same mechanism was at work. Was he afraid, even now, that Maigret might talk, that he had got himself mixed up in some serious business which would create all sorts of complications for him?

It was out of fear too that Pernelle, the recent new owner of the Clou Doré, had come to whisper in his ear the Rue de l'Étoile address. Fear of being harassed by the police in the future, fear of having his establishment closed down because of a breach of some obscure regulation.

Wasn't Monsieur Louis afraid too? Up until now he had remained in the shadows, with nothing explicitly linking him to Manuel and Aline. But now he too had the police snapping at his heels, and you don't live in Montmartre as long as he had without knowing what that means.

Who at this precise moment was most afraid, Aline or Fernand Barillard?

Only that morning, no one had any idea that there was a link between the two apartments on the fourth floor. Madame Barillard simply enjoyed her life without asking herself any questions, carrying out her housewifely duties to the best of her ability. Had Aline resigned herself to go to bed? Lucas remained stuck there like a limpet, calm and determined. Nothing would dislodge him. She couldn't go out and she couldn't make a telephone call. She suddenly found herself in her own company, cut off from the rest of the world. Wouldn't she rather have been taken to Quai des Orfèvres, where she could have protested and demanded a lawyer of her choice be present?

Officially, the police were only at her home for her protection.

Two doors and a landing separated her from the man she had received several times in her secret apartment at the Hôtel Bussière.

Was Palmari in the know? He too had lived for months with the police camped outside his home and his telephone tapped, and on top of all that, he was an invalid.

Yet he had continued to run his operation, directing his men via Aline as his go-between.

That was Maigret's last thought before he finally succumbed to sleep: Aline . . . Manuel . . . Aline called him Daddy . . . Snide and aggressive towards everyone else, she had a soft spot for the old gang leader and defended him like a tigress . . . Aline . . . Manuel . . .

Aline . . . Fernand . . .

There was someone missing. Maigret was no longer lucid enough to recall who was absent from the roll call.

One of the cogs. He had spoken about him to someone, maybe the magistrate? An important cog, because of the diamonds.

Aline . . . Manuel . . . Fernand . . . leave out Manuel, since he was dead . . . Aline . . . Fernand. Each of them in a cage, walking in circles, waiting for Maigret's next move.

When he woke up, Madame Maigret opened the window wide, then offered him a cup of coffee.

'Did you sleep well?'

'I don't know. I had lots of dreams, but I can't remember what they were about.'

The same sun as the day before, the same feeling of joy in the air, in the sky, in the chirruping of the birds, in the sounds and smells of the street.

It was Maigret who was different, who wasn't part of this happy chorus of the new day.

'You seem tired.'

'I have a big day ahead of me, some important decisions to make.'

She had guessed that the previous evening when he had come home, but she was careful not to ask any questions.

'Wear your grey pinstripe suit. It's lighter than the other one.'

Did he hear? He ate his breakfast mechanically and drank two cups of coffee without even tasting them. He didn't hum in the shower and got dressed with his mind elsewhere. He forgot to ask what was for lunch. His only question was:

'By the way, how was the lobster yesterday?'

'There's enough left to make a salad.'

'Call me a taxi, would you?'

No bus this morning, not even one with a platform. No passing scene, no coloured images to glide sensuously over his retina.

'Quai des Orfèvres!'

First, his office.

'Get me Fernand Barillard . . . Étoile 42.38 . . . Hello! Madame Barillard? . . . Detective Chief Inspector Maigret here . . . Could you put your husband on the line, please? . . . Yes, I can wait . . .'

He vaguely flicked through the pile of reports on his desk.

'Hello! . . . Barillard? . . . It's me again . . . I forgot yesterday to ask you to stay at home this morning and probably the rest of the day . . . I know! . . . I know! . . . You have clients expecting you, I'm sorry about that! . . . No, I have no idea what time I will be coming to see you . . .'

Lucas' report was simply a personal note for Maigret; he would write up his official report later.

Nothing important to report. She walked around the apartment until two o'clock in the morning, and more than once I wondered whether she was going to slap my face as she went past me. In the end she shut herself in her room, and after about half an hour it all went quiet in there. At eight o'clock, when Jarvis relieved me, she seemed to be sleeping. I'll ring into the office around eleven to see if you need me for anything.

Lapointe's report was not much more interesting. He had phoned in at three o'clock in the morning.

For the attention of Detective Chief Inspector Maigret.

Monsieur Louis and his companion stayed until eleven thirty at the Clou Doré. The girl is called Louise Pégasse, also known as Lulu the Torpedo, her stage name at the Boule Verte, a strip club on Rue Pigalle, where she tops the bill.

Monsieur Louis accompanied her there. I followed him and sat at a table near his. Lulu went in through the stage door and later reappeared to do her act, after which she installed herself at the bar, where, along with her colleagues, she has to encourage customers to buy drinks.

Monsieur Louis didn't move, didn't make a phone call. At no point did he leave the room. Just before three o'clock, Lulu walked over and whispered something in his ear. He went to collect his hat, and we waited out on the street, one behind the other. Lulu came out shortly afterwards. The pair of them then went on foot to a furnished hotel on Place Saint-Georges, the Hôtel du Square.

I questioned the night porter. Louise Pégasse has been living at the hotel for months. She often comes back with a man, rarely the same one. This was the second or third time Monsieur Louis had gone up to her room. I'm ringing from a bistro that's about to shut. I'll carry on with the stake-out.

'Janvier! Where's Janvier? Has he come in yet?'
'He's gone to the toilet, sir.'

'Send a man to relieve Lapointe outside the Hôtel du Square in Place Saint-Georges. He must be exhausted. If he has nothing new to report, tell him to go home and get some sleep and then ring in later this afternoon. It's possible I might need him again.'

He just had enough time to rush to the daily briefing, where he was the last to arrive, by some considerable margin. There were some knowing looks sent in his direction, for he had that expression on his face he wore on big days, grim, determined, pipe at an angle and clenched hard between his teeth: sometimes he had been known to bite it so hard he had snapped the ebonite stem.

'Apologies, commissioner.'

He didn't hear anything that the others said. When it came to his turn, he simply muttered:

'I am continuing my investigation into the death of Manuel Palmari. If all goes well, I hope to crack the jewel theft gang at the same time.'

'You're still pursuing that theory! How many years have you had Palmari under suspicion now?'

'Several years, I admit.'

There were some other reports awaiting his attention, the ones from Gastinne-Renette and the pathologist in particular. The three bullets that had hit Manuel, one of which had ended up lodged in the back of the wheelchair, had indeed been fired from Palmari's Smith & Wesson.

'Janvier! Can you come in here a moment?'

He gave him some instructions for organizing the guard duty at Rue des Acacias. A little later, he went to the Palais de Justice through the glass door that separates it from the Police Judiciaire. He had to go up two flights of stairs to get to the office of Examining Magistrate Ancelin, which was almost up in the rafters.

It was one of the unmodernized parts of the building which were allocated to new arrivals, and the magistrate had ended up having to pile his papers on the floor and keep his lamps on all day.

When he saw Maigret, the chubby magistrate rubbed his hands together.

'You can take a break,' he told his clerk. 'Sit down, my dear inspector. I'm keen to hear where things are at.'

Maigret gave him a summary of what he had been doing the previous day and of the reports he had received in the morning.

'Are you confident that all these disparate elements will add up to a coherent whole?'

'Each individual involved in this case is afraid. Each one of them is, right now, kept isolated from the others, with no means of communication . . .'

'I see! I see! Very crafty! On the other hand, not entirely by the book. I couldn't take such a course of action, but I'm beginning to understand your tactics. What will you do now?'

'First, I'll take a trip down to Rue La Fayette, where a diamond market takes place every morning in a bar and on the street. I know a few diamond dealers. It's somewhere I've visited on numerous occasions. Then I will head off to Gelot and Son, for reasons I am sure you can guess.'

'In short, if I have understood you correctly, the fact of the matter is this . . .'

And the magistrate, with a mischievous look in his eye, picked out the bones of the case, which proved he had spent part of the night studying the case file.

'I suppose you regard Palmari as the leader of the operation. Over the years, he has got to know crooks of all ages who have used his bar in Montmartre as a meeting place. The older generation has gradually dispersed throughout the country but has still preserved its contacts.

'In other words, with one well-placed phone call, Palmari could drum up the two or three men he needed for a given job. Right?'

Maigret nodded, amused by the magistrate's excitement.

'Even cut off from the world by his accident, nothing prevented him running his organization thanks to the help of Aline Bauche. He swiftly bought up the building where he lived with her, and I now wonder if he didn't have a particular reason for doing so.'

'Among other things, it allowed him to give certain tenants notice when he needed a vacant apartment.'

'For Barillard, for example. It's very handy having an accomplice on the same landing when you are being watched by the police. Do you think Barillard is capable of re-cutting gems and selling them on?'

'Selling them on, yes. Cutting them? No. It's one of the most expert jobs there is. Barillard identified the jewellers' shop windows that were worth raiding. That was very easy, given the work he does.

'He did this through Aline. And she sometimes gave us the slip and went to the Hôtel Bussière . . .'

'Hence the purchase of that hotel, which, apart from anything else, was a good investment.'

'Their accomplices would come up from the provinces for a day or two. Aline, or maybe Barillard, would wait for them at a predetermined location to take possession of the jewels.

'Mostly, the perpetrators of the heist were able to slip away without any difficulty, without even knowing on whose behalf they had pulled off the theft, which explains why so few of the crooks we arrested have been able to tell us anything.'

'In short, there is someone missing.'

'Precisely. The diamond cutter.'

'Good luck, Maigret. Can I call you that? Call me Ancelin.'

And Maigret replied with a smile:

'I'll try. In view of my relationships with previous examining magistrates, especially one called Coméliau, I fear I may not succeed at the first attempt. In the meantime, good day to you, sir. I will keep you posted.'

It was Gelot Junior who answered the phone when he rang the cardboard manufacturer on Avenue des Gobelins.

'No, no, Monsieur Gelot, nothing for you to worry about. I'm just making a few inquiries that have nothing to do with your firm. You say that Fernand Barillard is an excellent salesman, and I believe you.

'I simply wanted to know, for our information, the names of the jewellers who have placed orders with him in the last two years, say. I assume it will be easy for your accounts department to provide me with this list; I'll drop by later this morning to pick it up. Never fear. We know how to be discreet.'

In the inspectors' office he cast his gaze around all the faces in the room and in the end landed on Janvier, as usual.

'Doing anything important?'

'No, chief. I was finishing off a report, but it can wait. There's just so much paperwork.'

'Grab your hat and follow me.'

Maigret was of that generation which tended to resist learning to drive. In his case, he was worried about the way his mind would tend to wander into hazy reverie during the course of an investigation.

'The corner of Rue La Fayette and Rue Cadet.'

It was a principle of the police that when going off on an important mission you always took someone with you. If he hadn't had Lapointe with him the previous day at the Clou Doré, he wouldn't have been able to have Monsieur Louis followed, and it would no doubt have taken him several days to get on to the trail of Barillard.

'I'll find somewhere to park the car and then I'll join you.'

Like him, Janvier knew the gemstone market. Most Parisians, however, even those who pass through Rue La Fayette every day, have no idea that these unassuming-looking men, dressed like office clerks, chatting in groups on the pavement or around tables in the bar, have a fortune in precious stones in their pockets.

And these stones are passed from hand to hand in little bags, though no receipts are ever issued on the spot.

In this self-contained world, where everyone knows everyone, all transactions are based on trust.

'Hey, Bérenstein!'

Maigret shook hands with a tall, thin man who had just walked over from his two companions, having pocketed a bag of diamonds as if it were a simple letter.

'Hello, inspector. Another jewel robbery?'

'Not since last week.'

'You still haven't found who's responsible? I must have discussed it with my colleagues about two dozen times. Like me, they know all the stone cutters in Paris. As I've told you, there aren't many of them, and I can vouch for all of them. Not a single one of them would risk re-cutting stolen gems, or even any that are suspicious. They have a nose for this sort of thing, believe me! Will you have a beer with me?'

'Gladly. Once my inspector has crossed the road.'

'Hey! Janvier too! I see you're out in force today.'

They sat around a table, and between the rows some brokers stood talking. Occasionally one of them would take a magnifying glass out of his pocket to examine a stone.

'Before the war, the two main centres for stone cutting were Antwerp and Amsterdam. Curiously, for reasons I've never understood, most stone cutters come from the Baltic states, Latvia or Estonia.

'In Antwerp they had foreigners' identity cards, and when they retreated before the German advance, they were transferred as a group to Royan and then on to the United States.

'After the war, the Americans tried to hold on to them. But they barely managed to keep a tenth of them, because they were all homesick.

'Some of them, however, when they got back, succumbed to the lure of Paris. You'll find them in the Marais and Saint-Antoine districts. They are all well known and have their own pedigree, so to speak. It's a trade that gets passed down from father to son and it has its secrets.'

Maigret suddenly gave him a vague look, as if he wasn't listening any more.

'Wait. You mentioned . . .'

Something Bérenstein had said had struck him.

'What was it I said that's bothering you?'

'One moment! The German advance . . . The Antwerp stone cutters who . . . The United States . . . Some stayed over there . . . But mightn't some of them have stayed in France at the time of the exodus?'

'It's possible. As they were nearly all Jews they would have very likely ended up in concentration camps or the gas chambers.'

'Unless . . .'

Maigret suddenly stood up.

'Let's go, Janvier! Where's the car? Bye, Bérenstein. Excuse me. I should have thought of it earlier . . .'

And Maigret weaved his way through the groups filling the pavement as quickly as he could.

6.

Janvier stared straight in front of him, gripping the steering wheel of the little black car more tightly than usual, and he had to resist the temptation to observe the face of Maigret, who was sitting next to him. At one point he opened his mouth to ask a question that was preying on his mind, but he had enough self-control to remain silent.

Though he had worked with the chief ever since he had joined the Police Judiciaire and collaborated with him on hundreds of cases, he never failed to be impressed when he witnessed the phenomenon that had just been set in motion.

The previous day, Maigret had thrown himself into the case with a cheerful frenzy, drawing the protagonists out of the shadows, turning them over in his fat paws like a cat playing with a mouse and then putting them back in their corners. He was sending inspectors this way and that, as if he didn't have a plan, telling himself that something would emerge.

Then suddenly he wasn't playing any more. The man sitting next to Janvier was a whole different person now, a human mass on whom no one had any purchase, an almost frightening monolith. In the late morning, the avenues and streets of Paris were a veritable firework display in the July heat. There were splashes of light everywhere: glancing off the slate and red-tile roofs, the panes of windows where geraniums provided a single note of red, rippling across the many-coloured bodywork of cars – blues, greens, yellows – blaring horns, voices, the screech of brakes, bells, the piercing whistle of a policeman.

The black car was like an island of silence and immobility in the midst of this symphony, and Maigret himself was like an immovable object. He was certainly oblivious to the sights and sounds around him and didn't even notice that they had arrived at Rue des Acacias.

'We're here, chief.'

He struggled out of the car, which had become too narrow for him, gazed vacantly at the street, with which he was nonetheless very familiar, then lifted his head as if to take possession of the entire building, all its floors and all its inhabitants.

He paused to empty his pipe on the pavement by tapping it against his heel, and to fill another one and light it.

Janvier didn't ask him if he should accompany him; nor did he say a word to Janin, who was watching the building and wondering why the chief didn't seem to recognize him.

Maigret headed for the lift, followed by Janvier. Rather than press the button for the fourth floor, he chose the one for the fifth. Once there, he took long strides as he headed up to the garret.

Turning left, he stopped before the door of the deaf-mute and, knowing he would get no reply, he turned the doorknob. The door opened. The garret was empty.

Maigret almost ripped off the curtain of the wardrobe and made a brief inventory of the small number of mainly shabby clothes hanging there.

He took a mental snapshot of every corner of the room, after which he went back down to the floor below, hesitated, then took the lift back down to the ground floor. The concierge was in her lodge, a shoe on her right foot, a slipper on her left.

'Do you know if Claes went out this morning?'

Seeing him so tense made an impression on her.

'No, he hasn't been down yet.'

'Did you leave your lodge at any point?'

'Not even to sweep the stairs. A neighbour did it for me, because I've got my aches and pains again.'

'Did he go out last night?'

'No one went out. I only opened up for tenants coming home. Anyway, you've got an inspector outside who can tell you all that.'

Maigret was thinking strong and hard, to use the expression Janvier reserved for him alone.

'Tell me . . . Each tenant, if I understand correctly, has a part of the garret for their own personal use . . .'

'That's right. And in principle any of them can rent a room for a maid.'

'That's not what I asked. What about the cellar?'

'Before the war, there were only two large cellars, and everyone had their own spot for storing their coal. During the war, when anthracite became as expensive as caviar, there were lots of disputes, and some people claimed their own piles were going down rather too quickly. So the owner at the time built cubicles, each with its own door and padlock.'

'So each tenant has his own personal cellar?'

'Yes.'

'Including Claes?'

'No. He doesn't count as a proper tenant, since he lives in a maid's room.'

'And the Barillards?'

'Of course.'

'Do you have keys to the cellars?'

'No. I've just told you they have padlocks. Each tenant has his own.'

'Do you see who goes downstairs to the basement?'

'Not from here. The cellar stairs are opposite the service stairs at the back of the building. You just have to go through the door with no name on it and no doormat.'

Maigret went back to the lift and looked straight into Janvier's eyes without saying a word. He was too impatient to ring the Barillards' bell, but instead banged on the door with his fist. Madame Barillard answered in a cretonne dress, with a frightened expression on her face.

'Your husband?'

'He's in his study. He says you stopped him from going to work.'

'Call him.'

They could see Barillard's silhouette, still in pyjamas and dressing gown. Try as he might, he didn't seem as well or as self-assured as he had the day before.

'Bring me the key to the cellar.'

'But . . .'

'Do as I say.'

What followed had an air of unreality, as if it was a dream, or rather a nightmare. Suddenly, the relationships between them all shifted. It was as if everyone was now in a state of shock, and their words, gestures and looks all had a different meaning.

'Lead on.'

He pushed him into the lift and when they got to the ground floor ordered him tersely:

'To the basement.'

Barillard became more and more reluctant, Maigret more and more determined.

'Is it this door?'

'Yes.'

A single, very weak lightbulb illuminated the white wall, the doors with their painted numbers, now almost faded, and you could make out obscene graffiti on the flaking paintwork.

'How many keys are there to this padlock?'

'I only have one.'

'Who else might own a key?'

'How would I know?'

'Have you ever given the key to anyone else?'

'No.'

'Are you and your wife the only ones who access this cellar?'

'We haven't used it for years.'

'Open up.'

Barillard's hands were trembling, and his smart

appearance looked more grotesque down here than in the bourgeois confines of his apartment.

'Well? Open it!'

The door opened about fifteen centimetres then got stuck.

'I can feel something blocking it.'

'Push harder. Use your shoulder if necessary.'

Janvier was giving Maigret a bewildered look, suddenly realizing that his chief had foreseen – but since when? – the current turn of events.

'It's giving a little.'

Suddenly they saw a leg hanging. As the door swung further it released another leg. There was a body hanging there, bare feet dangling fifteen centimetres above the floor of beaten earth.

It was old Claes, dressed in a shirt and some old trousers.

'Put the 'cuffs on him, Janvier.'

Janvier looked from the hanged man to Barillard. When the salesman saw the handcuffs, he protested:

'Please, just a minute.'

But Maigret's unreadable gaze bore down on him, and he surrendered.

'Go and fetch Janin from the street. He is not needed outside any more.'

As he had done upstairs, Maigret inspected the long, narrow room, and it was evident that he was fixing every last detail in his mind. He fingered several tools that he took out of a bag, then seemed to dreamily caress a heavy steel table that was screwed into the floor.

'You stay here, Janin, until the gentlemen arrive. Don't let anyone in. Not even your colleagues. And don't touch a thing. Got that?'

'Got it, chief.'

'Let's go.'

He looked at Barillard, who cut a very different figure now with his hands behind his back and walking along like a mannequin.

They didn't take the lift but went up to the fourth floor via the back stairs, without bumping into anyone. Madame Barillard, who was in the kitchen, let out a cry when she saw her husband with handcuffs on his wrists.

'Monsieur Maigret!'

'Later, madame. First I have some telephone calls to make.'

And, paying no notice to the others, he went into Barillard's study, which smelled of stale cigarette smoke, and dialled the number of Examining Magistrate Ancelin.

'Hello! . . . Yes, Maigret here. I am an idiot, sir. I feel responsible for a man's death. Yes, another body. Where? Rue des Acacias, of course. It's something I should have realized from the start. I was hacking about in the undergrowth rather than following a clear single path. The worst thing is that this third element, if I can call it that, has been on my mind for years.

'Forgive me if I don't give any details right now. There is a hanged man in the cellar. The doctor will, I am sure, discover that he didn't hang himself but was dead or wounded when the rope was put round his neck. He is an old man.

'Could I ask you to arrange things so the prosecutor's office aren't on the case in too much of a hurry? I'm very busy on the fourth floor and would prefer not to be disturbed before I get a result. I don't know how long it will take. I'll speak to you later. Ah, no, we won't be having lunch at our nice Auvergnat bistro today.'

A short while later, he received a call from his old colleague Moers, the specialist from Criminal Records.

'I need to have a careful job done and I don't want it done quickly. No point in having the prosecutor's men and the magistrate tampering with things down in the cellar. You will find objects there that will surprise you. You might have to investigate the walls and dig up the floor.'

He got up from Barillard's chair with a sigh and walked across the living room to where Barillard sat facing Janvier, who was smoking a cigarette. Maigret went through to the kitchen and opened the fridge.

'May I?' he asked Madame Barillard.

'Tell me, inspector . . .'

'In a moment, if you don't mind. I'm dying of thirst.'

While he was taking the top off a bottle of beer, she handed him a glass, at once docile and afraid.

'Do you think my husband . . .'

'I don't think anything. Come with me.'

She followed him, bewildered, into the study, where he sat in Barillard's chair again without thinking.

'Sit down. Make yourself comfortable. Your maiden name is Claes, is it not?'

'Yes.'

She hesitated and started blushing.

'Look, inspector. I assume this is important?'

'From now onwards, madame, everything is important. You should know that everything you say matters.'

'I am indeed called Claes. It is the maiden name written on my identity card.'

'But?'

'I don't know if it is my real name.'

'Are you related to the man who lives in the garret?'

'I don't know. I don't think so. It was all so long ago. I was just a little girl.'

'What period are you talking about?'

'The bombing, in Douai, when we were fleeing the Germans. Train after train, where we had to get out and sleep on the ballast. Women carrying wounded babies. Men with armbands running all over the place and the train leaving again. Then the explosion, which sounded like the end of the world.'

'How old were you?'

'Four? Maybe a bit more or a bit less.'

'Where did the name of Claes come from?'

'I suppose it was the name of my family. At least, that's what I'm supposed to have said.'

'And the forename?'

'Mina.'

'Did you speak French?'

'No. Just Flemish. I'd never seen a town.'

'Can you remember the name of your village?'

'No. But why aren't you talking to me about my husband?'

'I'm getting there. Where did you meet the old man?'

'I'm not sure. Everything that happened immediately before and immediately after the explosion is confused in my memory. I seem to remember walking with someone holding my hand.'

Maigret picked up the phone and asked for the town hall in Douai. He was connected without having to wait.

'The mayor isn't here,' said the town clerk.

He was very surprised when Maigret asked him:

'How old are you?'

'Thirty-two.'

'And the mayor?'

'Forty-three.'

'Who was mayor when the Germans arrived in 1940?'

'Doctor Nobel. He remained mayor until ten years after the war.'

'Is he dead?'

'No. In spite of his age, he is still practising in his old house on the Grand Place.'

Three minutes later, Maigret had Doctor Nobel on the line, and Madame Barillard listened in amazement.

'Excuse me, doctor. Detective Chief Inspector Maigret from the Police Judiciaire. It's not about one of your patients, but about an old story that might throw light on more recent events. It was Douai station, wasn't it, that was bombed in broad daylight in 1940, when there were several refugee trains there and hundreds more refugees were waiting?'

Nobel hadn't forgotten – it had been the major event of his life.

'I was there, inspector. It is the most terrible memory a man can have. It was totally calm. The welcome committee was busy feeding the Belgian and French refugees whose trains were about to leave for the South.

'The women with babies were gathered together in the first-class waiting room, where they were provided with feeding bottles and fresh nappies. There were ten or so nurses helping out.

'In theory, no one was allowed to leave the train, but the attraction of refreshments was too strong. So there were people all over the place.

'Then suddenly, just as the sirens went off, the station shuddered, the glass shattered, and people started screaming, but it was impossible to work out what was going on.

'To this day we have no idea how many raids and how many waves of bombers there were.

'The scene outside was just as hallucinatory as that inside, in front of the station or on the platforms: bodies blown to bits, arms, legs, wounded people running round holding their chest or stomach, wild-eyed.

'I was lucky that I wasn't hit and I tried to turn the waiting room into a first-aid station. We didn't have enough ambulances, or enough hospital beds, to deal with all the wounded.

'I had to do emergency operations on the spot, in the most precarious conditions.'

'You probably don't remember a tall, thin man, a Fleming, who would have had his face cut open and who was left deaf and dumb.'

'Why do you want to know about him?'

'Because he's the one who interests me.'

'It just so happens, in fact, that I remember him very well and have often thought about him.

'I was there as mayor, as president of the local Red Cross and of the welcome committee and finally as a doctor.

'In my capacity as mayor, I tried to reunite families and identify those who had been badly wounded or killed, which wasn't always an easy task.

'Between you and me, we had to bury several bodies that we were unable to put a name to, in particular half a dozen old men who seemed to have come from a retirement home. Later, we tried to track down the home, but with no luck.

'In the midst of all this confusion and panic I remember one group very clearly: an entire family, an elderly man, two women, three or four children, who had literally been blown to bits.

'It was next to this group that I found the man, whose head was just a bloody mess, and I had him carried to a table, surprised that he was neither blind nor wounded in any vital organ.

'I can't tell you how many stitches I needed to sew him up. There was a little girl, unharmed, standing a short distance away, watching my every movement with no sign of emotion.

'I asked her if the man was a member of her family, her father or grandfather, but I don't know what she answered in Flemish.

'Half an hour later, as I was operating on a wounded

person, I saw the man back on his feet, heading for the exit, with the little girl following behind him.

'It was quite an amazing sight, in the middle of all this chaos. I had wrapped an enormous bandage round the man's head, but he seemed oblivious of it as he moved through the crowd; nor did he seem to pay much attention to the girl who trotted along at his heels.

' "Go and fetch them back," I called to one of my assistants. "He's in no fit state to wander off without further medical attention."

'That's basically all I can tell you, inspector. When I was able to think about him again, I tried to find out what had happened to him, but with no luck. He had been seen roaming among the debris and the ambulances. There was a continuous stream of vehicles of all sorts coming from the north, carrying furniture, families, mattresses, sometimes even pigs and cows.

'One of my scouts thought he saw a tall, elderly man, a little bent over, getting on board a military truck accompanied by a little girl, whom the soldiers helped to climb up.

'During and after the war, when we tried to restore some order to this chaos, many questions remained. Lots of the town halls in villages in Holland, Flanders and the Pas-de-Calais had been destroyed or looted, and the registers had been burned.

'Do you think you have found this man?'

'I'm almost certain that I have.'

'What became of him?'

'He has been found hanged, and at this moment I am sitting in front of that former little girl.'

'Will you tell me what happens?'

'As soon as everything becomes clear. Thank you, doctor.'

Maigret mopped his brow, emptied his pipe, filled another and said softly to the young woman:

'Now tell me your story.'

She had been watching him with wide, worried eyes, biting her nails, curled up in her chair like a little girl.

Rather than reply, she asked bitterly:

'Why do you treat Fernand like a criminal and why did you put handcuffs on him?'

'Can we talk about that later? For now, the best way you can help your husband is by answering my questions truthfully.'

She had another question on the tip of her tongue, a question she seemed to have had on her mind for a while, if not for ever.

'Was Jef mad? Jef Claes?'

'Did he act as if he were mad?'

'I don't know. I can't compare my childhood to anyone else's, or him to any other man.'

'Start with Douai.'

'Trucks, refugee camps, trains, policemen questioning the old man, because he seemed old to me, and then, when they couldn't get anything out of him, questioning me. Who were we? Which village did we come from? I didn't know.

'We went further, much further. I'm sure I saw the Mediterranean one time. I remembered it later and guessed we'd gone as far as Perpignan.'

'Was Claes trying to get to Spain? So he could get to America from there?'

'How would I have known? He couldn't hear or speak any more. To understand me, he would stare at my lips, and I had to repeat the same question over and over.'

'Why did he take you with him?'

'It was me. I've thought about it since then. I suppose that when I saw my family all dead around me I attached myself to the nearest man. Maybe he resembled my grandfather.'

'How come he took your name, assuming your name really is Claes?'

'I found that out later. He always had a few pieces of paper in his pocket and he sometimes wrote down some words in Flemish, because he still didn't speak French. Neither did I. In the end, after a few weeks or months, we washed up in Paris, and he rented a room and a kitchen in a district I've never managed to rediscover.

'He wasn't poor. Whenever he needed money he would reach under his shirt and take one or two gold coins that were sewn into a broad canvas girdle. These were his savings. We used to go well out of our way to find a jeweller's shop or a pawnbroker's, and he would enter furtively, afraid of being caught.

'I knew why the day the Jews were obliged to wear a yellow star sewn into their clothing. He wrote his real name on a piece of paper then burned it immediately: Victor Krulak. He was Jewish, from Latvia, born in Antwerp, where he worked in the diamond trade, like his father and grandfather before him.'

'Did you go to school?'

'Yes. The other children laughed at me.'

'Did Jef make your meals?'

'Yes. He was very good at grilled meats. He didn't wear a star. He was constantly afraid. They always gave him a hard time at the police station because he couldn't provide the necessary papers to acquire an identity card. One time they put him in an asylum somewhere because they thought he was mad, but he managed to escape the next day.'

'Was he fond of you?'

'I think he behaved that way because he didn't want to lose me. He had never been married. He didn't have any children. I'm sure he thought that God had meant for our paths to cross.

'We were twice sent back to the border, but we always returned to Paris and found a rented room with a small kitchen, sometimes around Sacré-Cœur, sometimes in the Saint-Antoine neighbourhood.'

'Did he work?'

'Not at this time.'

'How did he spend his days?'

'He wandered around, watched people, learned how to read their lips, how to understand their language. One day, towards the end of the war, he came home with a false identity card, which he had been trying to get hold of for four years.

'He was now officially Jef Claes, and I was his grand-daughter.

'We lived in slightly more spacious lodgings, not far

from the Hôtel de Ville, and people came to see him to give him work. I wouldn't be able to recognize them now.

'I went to school. I grew up and became a sales assistant in a jeweller's on Boulevard Beaumarchais.'

'Did old Jef find you the position?'

'Yes. He did odd jobs for different jewellers – repairs and restoration of old jewels.'

'Is that how you met Barillard?'

'A year later. As a sales representative he only needed to visit us every three months, but he came more often and in the end would wait for me at the door of the shop. He was handsome, very jolly and lively. He loved life. It was with him that I drank my first aperitif, at the Quatre Sergents de la Rochelle.'

'Did he know you were Jef's granddaughter?'

'I told him. I described our whole adventure to him. Since he intended to marry me, he naturally asked to be introduced. We got married and went to live in a house in Fontenay-sous-Bois, taking Jef with us.'

'Did you ever meet Palmari?'

'Our former neighbour? I couldn't say, because all the time we have lived here I've never seen him. Fernand would sometimes bring friends home, charming men who liked a good laugh and a good drink.'

'And the old man?'

'He spent most of his time in a tool shed at the bottom of the garden, where Fernand had set up a workshop for him.'

'Did you ever suspect anything?'

'Why would I suspect anything?'

'Tell me, Madame Barillard, is your husband in the habit of getting up during the night?'

'Virtually never.'

'Does he ever leave the apartment.'

'Why?'

'Before you go to bed, do you have some sort of herbal tea?'

'A verbena, sometimes a camomile.'

'Did you wake up last night?'

'No.'

'Would you show me your bathroom?'

This wasn't very big, but it was quite bright and charming, with yellow tiles. There was a medicine cabinet recessed into the wall above the sink. Maigret opened it, examined a few small bottles and kept one in his hand.

'Are these your pills?'

'I don't even know what they are. They've been there for ages. Oh, I remember! Fernand suffers from insomnia, and a friend of his recommended these pills.'

But the label was new.

'What's going on, inspector?'

'What's going on is that last night, and on a number of previous nights, you have without knowing it been taking a certain quantity of this drug in your tea, which has made you sleep deeply. Your husband went up to find Jef in his garret and took him down to the cellar.'

'The cellar?'

'Where he has set up a workshop. He hit him with a piece of lead piping or some other similar object and then hanged him from the ceiling.'

She let out a cry but didn't faint. Instead, she ran into the living room and screamed at her husband:

'Is this true, Fernand? Is it true that you did that to old Jef?'

Oddly enough, she had fully regained her Flemish accent.

Before the scene became overcharged, Maigret led Barillard into the study and signalled to Janvier to keep an eye on the young woman. The previous evening the two men had found themselves in the same study, but they had now swapped places. Today it was the inspector who sat in Barillard's revolving chair and the latter who sat facing him, less abrasive than at their previous interview.

'It's cowardly.'

'What is cowardly, Barillard?'

'Picking on a woman. If you had questions to ask, why not ask me directly?'

'I have no questions to ask you, because I already know the answers. You guessed that after our conversation yesterday, since you decided it was necessary to eliminate once and for all the weak link in your organization.

'After Palmari, Victor Krulak, known as Jef Claes. A poor man who was mentally confused and who would have done anything not be separated from the little girl who had placed her hand in his on Judgement Day. You bastard.'

'Thanks very much.'

'There are crooks and then there are crooks. Some I would shake by the hand, like Palmari, for example. But you, you are of the lowest sort, the ones you can't look in the face without wanting to hit them or spit.'

And indeed, Maigret really had to restrain himself.

'Carry on! I'm sure my lawyer will be delighted to hear all this.'

'In a few minutes, you will be taken to the police cells and, this afternoon probably, we will continue our conversation.'

'With my lawyer present.'

'But first, there is someone to whom I owe a visit which may take some time. I think you know who I'm talking about. And the result of this visit will to a large extent determine your fate.

'With Palmari out of the way, there are now only two people at the summit of this pyramid: Aline and you.

'I now know that you were going to abscond together at the first opportunity, once you had got your hands on Manuel's hoard on the sly.

'Aline . . . Fernand . . . Aline . . . Fernand . . . When I have you in front of me again, I will know which of you two is – I won't say the guilty party, since you both are – but let's say the true instigator of these murders. Got that?'

Maigret called out:

'Janvier! Could you escort the gentleman to the cells? He is allowed to get properly dressed, but don't let him out of your sight for an instant. Are you armed?'

'Yes, chief.'

'It must be crawling with police officers downstairs. Find one to accompany you. See you later.'

On the way out, he stopped in front of Madame Barillard.

'Please don't blame me, madame, for your current pain and the pain you are still to suffer.'

'Did Fernand kill him?'

'I'm afraid that is the case.'

'But why?'

'You will have to get your head round it sooner or later: because your husband is a crook, you poor woman. And because he found a female counterpart in the apartment across the way.'

He left her in tears and a few moments later was down in the cellar, where the yellow lightbulb had been replaced by spotlights. It was like walking on to a film set.

Everyone was talking at once. Photographers were taking pictures. The doctor with the bald head was asking for silence, and Moers was unable to reach Maigret.

The little magistrate found himself next to Maigret, who dragged him out into the open air.

'A glass of beer, sir?'

'I wouldn't say no, if I could get through.'

They slipped through with great difficulty. The death of the relatively unknown Jef had not passed as unnoticed as that of Manuel Palmari, and a crowd had gathered outside the building which two policemen were struggling to contain. Some reporters started following Maigret.

'No comment this morning, boys. After three o'clock, back at HQ.'

He led his stout companion to Chez l'Auvergnat, where

some regulars were already having lunch and the air was cooler.

'Two large beers.'

'Are you on top of all this, Maigret?' the magistrate asked, mopping his brow. 'It seems that they are discovering a lot of up-to-date diamond-cutting equipment in the cellar. Were you expecting that?'

'I've been looking for it for twenty years.'

'Seriously?'

'Very much so. I knew how all the other pawns moved. Cheers!'

He drained his glass slowly, put it down on the bar and murmured:

'Same again.'

Then, still with a hard expression:

'I should have understood everything yesterday. Why didn't I remember that business in Douai? I sent my men scurrying off in all directions except the right one, and when it finally dawned on me, it was too late.'

He watched the landlord pour him another beer. He was breathing heavily, like a man holding himself in check.

'What are you going to do now?'

'I sent Barillard to the cells.'

'Have you interrogated him?'

'No. It's too early. I have someone else I need to question before him, now, straight away.'

He looked out of the window at the building opposite, in particular at a certain window on the fourth floor.

'Aline Bauche?'

'Yes.'

'At her place?'

'Yes.'

'Wouldn't she be more subdued in your office?'

'Nothing subdues her.'

'Do you think she'll confess?'

Maigret shrugged his shoulders, thought about ordering another beer, decided against it and offered his hand to the little magistrate, who looked at him with both admiration and a certain disquiet.

'See you later. I'll keep you posted.'

'I think I'll have lunch here and as soon as they have finished up across the road I'll go back to the Palais.'

He didn't dare add: 'Good luck!'

Maigret, his shoulders slumped, went back across the road, looking up once more to the window on the fourth floor. They let him pass, and just one photographer had the presence of mind to take a snap of the inspector marching resolutely ahead.

7.

When Maigret knocked noisily on the door of what used to be Manuel Palmari's apartment he heard irregular footsteps approaching on the inside, and it was Inspector Janin who opened, looking, as usual, as if he had been caught in the act. Janin was a scrawny fellow, and his left leg splayed outwards when he walked. He was like one of those dogs that always anticipates being hit.

Was he afraid that Maigret would reproach him for taking off his jacket and having his dubious shirt unbuttoned over his skinny, hairy chest?

Maigret barely gave him a glance.

'Has anyone used the telephone?'

'Just me, chief, to tell my wife . . .'

'Have you had lunch?'

'Not yet.'

'Where is she?'

'In the kitchen.'

And Maigret frowned again. The apartment was a mess. In the kitchen, Aline was smoking a cigarette in front of a plate containing the congealing remains of some fried eggs. The woman sitting here had little in common with the spruce, well-buffed 'little lady' who dressed with great care every morning before going to do her shopping.

She was probably wearing nothing but that blue silk dressing gown, which was sticking to her skin because of the sweat. Her dark hair was unbrushed, she was wearing no make-up. She hadn't bathed and was emitting a tangy odour.

It wasn't the first time Maigret had encountered this phenomenon. He had known several women as stylish and well groomed as Aline had been who, left to their own devices after the deaths of their husbands, had similarly let themselves go virtually overnight.

Their tastes and attitudes changed suddenly. They dressed more gaudily, spoke in a more vulgar manner, adopting a language they had tried hard to suppress, as if their natural tendencies were regaining the upper hand.

'Come.'

She knew Maigret well enough to realize that this time the game was deadly serious. Nevertheless, she took her time getting up, stubbed out her cigarette on the greasy plate, put the packet in her dressing-gown pocket and went to the fridge.

'Are you thirsty?' she asked hesitantly.

'No.'

She didn't insist but got a bottle of cognac and a glass for herself from the cupboard.

'Where are you taking me?'

'I told you to come here, with or without the cognac.'

He made her walk across the living room and pushed her none too gently into Palmari's little room, where the wheelchair still stood as a reminder of the old gang leader.

'Sit down, lie down or stay standing . . .' Maigret

muttered as he took off his jacket and looked for a pipe in the pocket.

'What's happened?'

'What's happened is, it's all over. It's time to settle accounts. You understand that, don't you?'

She had sat on the edge of the yellow sofa, her legs crossed, and with trembling hands she tried to light the cigarette she held between her lips.

She didn't care that she was exposing part of her thighs. Maigret didn't care either. Whether she was clothed or naked, the time when she could tempt a man had passed.

Maigret was witnessing a sort of collapse. He had known her when she was quite sure of herself, often arrogant, mocking him with a sharp tongue or insulting him in terms that led to Manuel ticking her off.

He had known her as a natural beauty, still with a whiff of the street about her, which added a certain spicy quality.

He had known her in tears, as a grief-stricken woman or as an actress playing that role so well that he had let himself be taken in by it.

Now she was just a cornered animal, crouching, smelling of fear and wondering what fate had in store for her.

Maigret fiddled with the wheelchair, turning it this way and that, then finally sat down on it in the pose in which he had so often seen Palmari.

'He lived here three years, a prisoner of this instrument.'

He was talking as if to himself, his hands pressing the buttons that made it turn left and right.

'You were his only way of communicating with the outside world.'

She turned her head away, disturbed by seeing someone of the same build as Manuel sitting in his chair. Maigret carried on talking, as if unconcerned about her.

'He was an old-school gangster, a "daddy" gangster. And those old guys were wary in a different way from the younger generation. In particular, they never allowed women to be involved in their business, except to pimp them out for profit. Manuel had moved beyond that stage. Are you listening?'

'I'm listening,' she stammered like a little girl.

'The truth of the matter is that, late in life, the old crocodile fell in love with you like a schoolboy with a crush, fell in love with a girl he picked up outside some sleazy hotel on Rue Fontaine.

'He had saved up a hoard of cash that would have enabled him to retire to the banks of the Marne or somewhere in the South.

'The poor sucker thought he would be able to turn you into a real lady. He dressed you in fine clothes. He taught you how to be presentable. He didn't need to teach you how to count, since you had learned that in the womb.

'And how affectionate you were with him! Daddy this and Daddy that. Are you feeling OK, Daddy? Do you want me to open a window? Are you thirsty, Daddy? Can your little Aline give you a kiss?'

He stood up suddenly and growled:

'You bitch!'

She didn't flinch, didn't move a muscle. She knew that

in anger he was quite capable of slapping or even punching her in the face.

'Was it you who persuaded him to put the properties in your name? And the bank accounts? It doesn't matter! While he was stuck here within these four walls you were out meeting his accomplices, giving them instructions, picking up the diamonds. Do you still have nothing to say?'

The cigarette slipped from her fingers, and she stubbed it out on the carpet with the tip of her slipper.

'How long have you been the mistress of that strutting peacock Fernand? A year, three years, a few months? The hotel on Rue de l'Étoile was very handy for your trysts.

'Then, one day, one of you, Fernand or you, got impatient. Even in his much-diminished state, Manuel was in stable health and could have gone on for another ten or fifteen years.

'He had enough put away that he could think about ending his days somewhere else, where he could be taken out into the garden and feel in contact with nature.

'Was it you or Fernand who couldn't bear the thought of that? Now it's your turn to speak, and be quick about it.'

With a heavy tread he walked from one window to the other, glancing occasionally at the street below.

'I'm listening.'

'I've got nothing to say.'

'Was it you?'

'It was nothing to do with me.'

Then, with a great deal of effort:

'What have you done with Fernand?'

'He's in the cells, stewing in his own juices, waiting for me to interrogate him.'

'Has he said anything?'

'It doesn't matter what he has said. Let me put this to you a different way. You didn't kill Manuel with your own hands, I get that. Fernand took care of that while you were out shopping. As for the second murder . . .'

'What second murder?'

'You really don't know that there has been another death in the building?'

'Who?'

'Come on! Think about it, unless this is just an act. Palmari is out of the picture. But Barillard, whom no one has ever suspected, finds himself all of a sudden under investigation by the police.

'Instead of bringing you both into Quai des Orfèvres and putting you face to face, we left you each in your own cage, you here, him over the hallway with his wife, with no links to the outside world and no means of communicating with each other.

'And what happens then? You wander around from your bed to your chair, and from your chair to the kitchen, nibbling at bits of food and not even bothering to wash.

'He is wondering how much we know. Above all, he is wondering who could have given evidence against him that put him in the frame. Rightly or wrongly, he is not worried that you will talk. But upstairs, in the garret, there is a stooge who might be not quite right in the head, who might be more cunning than he lets on and who might snitch.'

'Old Jef is dead?' she stammered.

'You didn't think he'd be first on the list, did you?'

She stared at him, completely thrown, looking for something to cling to.

'How?'

'He was found hanged this morning in Barillard's cellar, a cellar which was long ago converted into a workshop where Jef Claes, or more accurately Victor Krulak, re-cut stolen gems.

'He didn't hang himself. He was fetched from upstairs, taken down to the cellar, where he was killed before having a noose put round his neck.'

He spoke slowly and didn't look the young woman in the face.

'Now it is no longer a matter of burglaries, precious stones or sleeping together at the Hôtel Bussière. It's a matter of two murders, rather two assassinations, committed in cold blood, with premeditation. One of you at least has your head on the line.'

Unable to sit still any longer, she stood up and started walking round in turn, taking care not to pass too near to Maigret.

'What do you think?' he heard her murmur.

'That Fernand is a wild animal and you became his mate. That you lived here for months and years with a man you called Daddy and who trusted you, and the whole time you were just waiting for the moment when you could hop into bed with that lowlife.

'You must have each been as impatient as the other. It hardly matters who actually held the gun that killed Manuel.'

'It wasn't me.'

'Sit down here.'

He pointed to the wheelchair, and she stiffened, her eyes like saucers.

'Sit down here!'

Suddenly he grabbed her arm and forced her to sit down where he wanted her to.

'Don't move. I want you to sit in the exact spot where Manuel spent the vast majority of his day. Here! With the radio within reach of one hand, magazines in reach of the other. That's right, isn't it?'

'Yes.'

'And where was the gun, which Manuel never went anywhere without?'

'I don't know.'

'You're lying, because you saw Palmari put it there every morning after having it with him all night in his bedroom. Is that correct?'

'Maybe.'

'There's no "maybe" about it, for God's sake! It's the truth! You forget that I've been here twenty, thirty times to talk to him.'

She sat frozen in the chair where Manuel had died, her face drained of colour.

'Now listen carefully. You left to do your shopping, all dressed up, after giving Daddy a kiss on the forehead and a parting smile as you went through the door of the living room.

'Let's assume that at this point the gun was still in its place behind the radio. Fernand came in using his key – because he had his own key, which allowed him to make contact with the chief whenever he needed to.

'Look around at the furniture. Can you imagine Fernand walking round the chair and slipping his hand behind the radio to take hold of the gun and fire a first bullet into Manuel's neck?

'No, my dear. Palmari wasn't born yesterday and he'd have been suspicious from the very first movement.

'The truth, you see, is that when you kissed Daddy, when you smiled at him, when you skipped out, very much the neat and pretty young lady, wiggling your little behind, the gun was stashed inside your handbag.

'It was all choreographed. On the landing, you just had to slip it into the hand of Fernand, who was coincidentally leaving his apartment at the same moment.

'While you entered the lift and headed off to do your shopping, some nice red meat and vegetables still with an earthy smell about them, he stayed in his apartment until the prearranged time.

'So no need now to squeeze past the old man's chair and slip a hand between him and the radio.

'Just one quick movement, after an exchange of words. I know what care Manuel took of his weapons. The gun was well oiled, and I'm sure we will find traces of the oil in your bag.'

'It's not true!' she cried, throwing herself at Maigret and battering his shoulders and face with her fists. 'I didn't kill him! It was Fernand! He did everything! It was all his idea!'

Maigret didn't bother to parry the blows. He just called out:

'Janin! Will you take care of her?'

'Shall I 'cuff her?'

'Just until she calms down. Here! Let's put her on this sofa. I'll send you up something to eat and I'll try to get some lunch myself. Later she will have to get dressed, or we will have to make her get dressed ourselves.'

8.

'A beer for starters.'

The little restaurant still smelled of lunch, but the paper tablecloths had disappeared, and there was only one customer in the corner, reading the paper.

'Could you ask your waiter to take two or three sandwiches to the fourth floor, left-hand apartment, in the building opposite, as well as a carafe of wine?'

'And you? Have you had lunch? All finished over there?

'Would you like some sandwiches too? Some Cantal ham?'

Maigret felt damp under his clothes. His huge body was empty, his limbs were limp. He felt a bit like someone who has been battling a raging fever, which had suddenly relented.

For hours he had been forging ahead, oblivious to the familiar scenery around him, and he would have been hard put to even remember what day it was. He was surprised to see the clock showing two thirty.

What had he forgotten? He was vaguely aware that he had missed a meeting with someone. But who? Ah, yes! Gelot Junior on Avenue des Gobelins, who would have drawn up that list of jewellers visited by Fernand Barillard.

Things had moved on apace since then. The list would prove useful later, and Maigret imagined the little examining magistrate in the subsequent weeks summoning witness after witness to his messy office and compiling an ever-thickening file.

The world around Maigret was starting to return to life. He heard the sounds of the street once more, noticed the reflections of the sunlight and slowly relished the taste of his sandwich.

'Is this wine any good?'

'A little harsh for some tastes. That's because it hasn't been tampered with. It comes direct from my brother-in-law's place; he only produces about twenty bottles a year.'

He tasted some of the wine that he had sent up to Janin and, when he left the restaurant, he no longer seemed like a raging bull.

'When is my house going to get back to normal?' the concierge lamented as he walked in.

'Soon, soon, my dear lady.'

'Should I still be paying the rent money to the young lady?'

'I don't think so. The examining magistrate will decide.'

The lift took him up to the fourth floor. First, he rang at the door on the right, and Madame Barillard opened to him, her eyes red, still dressed in the flowery dress she was wearing that morning.

'I've come to say goodbye, Mina. Forgive me for calling you that, but I can't help thinking of that little girl in the hell of Douai who placed her hand in the hand of a man with a bloody face walking straight ahead who didn't know where he was going. You didn't know where he was taking you either.'

'Is it true, inspector, that my husband is . . .'

She couldn't bring herself to say it: a murderer.

He nodded.

'You are still young, Mina. Don't despair!'

Madame Barillard managed to murmur through her swollen lips:

'How come I didn't notice anything?'

Suddenly she threw herself against Maigret's chest, and he let her cry her eyes out. One day, no doubt, she would find a new support, another hand to hang on to.

'I promise to come back and see you. Take care of yourself. Life goes on.'

Across the landing, Aline was sitting on the edge of the sofa.

'We're leaving,' announced Maigret. 'Do you want to get dressed or would you rather go as you are?'

She looked at him as if she had been doing a lot of thinking and had come to a decision.

'Will I see him?'

'Yes.'

'Today?'

'Yes.'

'Will I be able to talk to him?'

'Yes.'

'As much as I like?'

'As much as you like.'

'Am I allowed to have a shower?'

'Provided you leave the bathroom door open.'

She shrugged her shoulders. What did it matter if she was seen or not? For almost an hour she attended to her ablutions, perhaps more meticulously than she had ever done in her life before.

She took the trouble to wash her hair and dry it with an electric hairdryer and dithered for a long while before choosing a black satin suit with a severe cut.

The whole time she remained steely-eyed and wore a determined expression.

'Janin! Go downstairs and see if there is a car available.'

'On my way, chief.'

For a moment, Maigret and the young woman found themselves alone in the living room. She slipped on her gloves. The sun flooded in through the two windows, which were open on to the street.

'Admit that you had a soft spot for Manuel,' she murmured.

'In a way, yes.'

And instantly she added, without looking at him:

'For me too, no?'

And he repeated:

'In a way.'

After this, he opened the door, closed it again behind them and put the key in his pocket. They took the lift down. There was an inspector waiting in a black car. Janin stood on the pavement, not knowing what to do.

'Go home and sleep for ten hours solid.'

'Assuming my wife and kids let me sleep that long! Thanks anyway, chief.'

Vacher was driving the car, and Maigret had a few quiet words in his ear. He then sat down next to Aline in the back seat. When they had gone about a hundred metres, the young woman, who had been staring out of the window, turned towards him.

'Where are we going?'

Instead of taking the most direct route back to Quai des Orfèvres, they were heading down Avenue de la Grande-Armée, around Place de l'Étoile and on to the Champs-Élysées.

She was absorbing the whole spectacle, knowing that there was every chance that she would never see it again, or rather that if she did, she would be a very old woman.

'Did you do it on purpose?'

Maigret sighed but didn't reply. Twenty minutes later, she followed him into his office; he was evidently pleased to be back on home turf.

Mechanically, he tidied up his pipes, walked over to the window and then finally opened the door to the inspectors' room.

'Janvier!'

'Yes, chief?'

'Could you go down to the cells and bring Barillard up here? Take a seat, Aline.'

He was now behaving as if nothing had happened. He gave the impression that he wasn't involved any more, that the whole case had been a mere interlude in his life.

'Hello! Could you put me through to Examining Magistrate Ancelin, please? Hello! . . . Hello! . . . Yes sir, Maigret here. Back at the office, yes. I've just returned with a young woman of your acquaintance. No, but it won't be long now. I wonder if you would like to be here for the confrontation. Yes. Straight away. See you very soon.'

He thought about taking his jacket off but decided against it, because of the magistrate.

'Nervous?'

'What do you think?'

'That we're about to witness a fight between two wild animals.'

The woman's eyes flashed.

'If you were armed I wouldn't much fancy his chances.'

The jolly little magistrate arrived first and looked curiously at the young woman in black, who had just sat down.

'Take my chair, sir.'

'I wouldn't want to . . .'

'Please, I insist. My role is almost over. We only need to check some things, interview a few witnesses, write our reports and send them to you. A week of paperwork.'

They heard footsteps in the corridor, and Janvier knocked on the door and pushed Fernand, in handcuffs, into the office.

'As for these two, they're all yours now.'

'Shall I take the 'cuffs off, chief?'

'I don't think that would be wise. As for you, stay here. I'll make sure we've got some muscle next door.'

Aline had become alert and seemed to sniff the scent of the man who had been her long-time lover.

Not her lover, her mate. Just as she had been his.

They were two animals looking at each other, in this quiet office, as if they were sizing each other up in a bear pit or in the jungle.

Their lips trembled, their nostrils contracted. Fernand hissed:

'What have you . . .'

Sat opposite him, her back arched, her muscles taut, she thrust forward a hate-filled face and spat in his face.

Without wiping himself, he took a step forwards too, hands outstretched, threateningly, while the little magistrate fidgeted uncomfortably in Maigret's chair.

'You bitch, you . . .'

'Bastard! . . . Thug! . . . Murderer!'

She managed to scratch his face, but, in spite of the handcuffs, he grabbed her arm in mid-air and twisted it, leaning over her with his eyes full of all the hatred in the world.

Maigret, standing in the doorway to the inspectors' office, made a sign, and two men dashed in to separate the pair, who were now rolling about on the floor.

For a few moments there was a confused scuffle, and finally Barillard was hauled to his feet, his face bloodied, while Aline was also handcuffed and pushed towards a chair.

'I think it will be fine to question them separately, sir. The hard thing won't be getting them to speak, it will be getting them to shut up.'

Louis Ancelin got up, led Maigret to the window and, still shaken by what he had just seen, murmured in his ear:

'I've never witnessed such an outpouring of hate, such raw animality!'

Over his shoulder, Maigret called to Janvier:

'You can lock them up!'

And he added ironically:

'Separately, of course.'

He didn't watch them leave but gazed out over the peacefully flowing Seine. He was looking for a familiar figure on the riverbank, an angler. He had called him 'his' angler for years, even though it was unlikely to be the same person. But the only thing that mattered was that there was always someone fishing next to Pont Saint-Michel.

A tug pulling four barges sailed upstream and lowered its funnel to pass under the stone arch of the bridge.

'Tell me, Maigret, which one of them, in your opinion . . .'

Maigret took the time to light his pipe before he spoke, still gazing out of the window:

'You're the magistrate, aren't you? I can only hand them over to you just as they are.'

'It wasn't a pretty sight.'

'No, it wasn't a pretty sight. Neither was Douai.'

OTHER TITLES IN THE SERIES

MAIGRET AND THE SATURDAY CALLER
GEORGES SIMENON

'I followed you. Last Saturday, I nearly came up to you in the street, then I thought that wasn't the right place. Not for the kind of conversation I wanted to have. Not in your office either. Perhaps you'll understand . . .'

When Maigret is followed home by a man who confesses he intends to commit a crime, he tries to dissuade this strange visitor, but a subsequent disappearance casts an ominous new light on events.

Translated by Sian Reynolds

INSPECTOR MAIGRET

OTHER TITLES IN THE SERIES

MAIGRET AND THE TRAMP
GEORGES SIMENON

'Maigret was devoting as much of his time to this case as he would to a drama keeping the whole of France agog. He seemed to be making it a personal matter, and from the way he had just announced his encounter with Keller, it was almost as if he was talking about someone he and his wife had been anxious to meet for a long time.'

When a Paris tramp known as 'Doc' is pulled from the Seine after being badly beaten, Maigret must delve into the past to discover who wanted to kill this mysterious figure.

Translated by Howard Curtis

OTHER TITLES IN THE SERIES

MAIGRET'S ANGER
GEORGES SIMENON

'There was a dressing table painted grey and cluttered with jars of cream, make-up, eyeliner. The room had a stale, faintly sickly smell. This was where the performers swapped their everyday clothes for their professional gear before stepping out into the spotlights, out to where men bought champagne at five or six times the going rate for the privilege of admiring them.'

Maigret is perplexed by the murder of a Montmartre nightclub owner, until he uncovers a crime much closer to home that threatens his own reputation.

Translated by Will Hobson

INSPECTOR MAIGRET

OTHER TITLES IN THE SERIES

MAIGRET AND THE GHOST
GEORGES SIMENON

'It wasn't a traditional painter's smock that Madame Jonker was wearing. It was more a monk's habit, the fabric as thick and soft as a bathrobe.

The Dutchman's wife also wore a white turban of the same fabric around her head.

She was holding a palette in her left hand, a brush in her right, and her black eyes lighted on Maigret with curiosity.'

The shooting of a fellow inspector and the disappearance of a key witness lead Maigret to some disturbing discoveries about an esteemed Paris art critic.

Translated by Ros Schwartz

OTHER TITLES IN THE SERIES

MAIGRET DEFENDS HIMSELF
GEORGES SIMENON

*'Maigret's cheeks turned red, as they had at school whenever he was called
to the headmaster's office. 28 June ... He had been in the Police Judiciaire for
more than thirty years, and the head of the Crime Squad for ten years, but
this was the first time he had been summoned like this.'*

When Maigret is shocked to find himself accused of a crime, he
must fight to prove his innocence and save his reputation.

Translated by Howard Curtis

OTHER TITLES IN THE SERIES

And more to follow